The Angel of Time

Michael Stewart

Copyright

Dedication

This book is dedicated to my Great Grandfather, William Puttnam who served in the Royal Field Artillery through all of the great battles on the Western Front from August 1915 to March 1918 when he was eventually wounded on the Somme. Also to his hard working and loving wife, Amy Louise, who single-handedly managed to bring up their six children during the war, including my Grandmother Violet.

The story of our own hero George, from his wounding at the Somme, his long and arduous evacuation across France, England and then onto Scotland before his eventual return home is based upon the true events as experienced by my Great Grandfather in 1918. Without the efforts of these good, honest, hardworking people, and many others like them, I would not be here and this story would not have been told.

Contents

Copyright

Dedication

Contents

Chapter One - Somewhere in No-Man's-Land, France 23 March 1918

Chapter Two - Berkhampsted, Hertfordshire, England - April 1984

Chapter Three - Bapaume, France - 23 March 1918

Chapter Four - Rouen, France - 27 March 1918

Chapter Five - SS Saint Patrick - 28 March 1918

Chapter Six - Malbork Castle, Prussia - 27 March 1918

Chapter Seven - Southampton, Hampshire, England - 28 March 1918

Chapter Eight - Merryflats Hospital, Glasgow, Scotland - 29 March 1918

Chapter Nine - Colmworth, Bedfordshire, England - 6 September 1918

Chapter Ten - Going Home - 10 October 1918

Chapter Eleven - Berkhampsted, Hertfordshire, England - 18 November 1918

Chapter Twelve - Berkhampsted, Hertfordshire, England - 11 July 1919

Chapter Thirteen - Ducks Cross Camp, Colmworth, England - 1 June 1920

Chapter Fourteen - Berkhampsted, Hertfordshire, England - 2 June 1920

Chapter Fifteen - Epilogue – December 1945

A thank you from the Author

Chapter One

Somewhere in No-Man's-Land, France 23 March 1918

The two soldiers crept as silently as possible through the thick cloying mud and other debris of war. The night was pitch black but the stars were so close and bright their night adjusted eyes could see well enough. Their green and grey woollen uniforms blended well with the mud and the darkness and with their faces blackened, the two soldiers were virtually invisible. They picked their way from shell hole to shell hole towards the enemy lines. The men of the Jäger Division were perhaps the best, certainly the youngest and the fittest, and they were often picked for the night time patrols. Their aim was to try to get as close to the enemy lines as possible to pick up any information they could, or even better, to pick up a Tommy or two as a prisoner whom they could take back to their own lines and interrogate. The patrols were scattered all along the front line in this sector, operating quietly in pairs during the dead of night, only dropping down to hug the mud when a flare went up from the trenches. They knew the deadly British sharpshooters were watching.

As they came to the top of one deep shell-hole the pair stopped and crouched down at the command of the man at the rear. All was deathly silent except for the occasional cough which could be heard from the trenches in front of them. The man in front turned back to his partner to see what he might have spotted. All he saw was his comrade's Luger pistol aimed at his head.

'Sorry it has to be this way,' was the last thing he heard from his partner as the gun went off. The pain exploded in his head instantly. His world went black and the soldier fell headfirst down into the mud filled shell hole.

Chapter Two

Berkhampsted, Hertfordshire, England - April 1984

I guess there have been at least three life changing moments in my relatively short and otherwise fairly mundane life so far. Being born was certainly the first of them, being dumped by my parents before my first birthday was probably the second, and the third was definitely the day I finally left Gade House - my home for 15 troubled years. Gade House was what is most usually referred to as an orphanage, a children's home or as in my case, a home for unwanted children. I didn't realise it that morning, but today was to see the fourth and certainly the most significant life changing event of all.

With the hood of my tatty brown duffel coat covering my head and my hands shoved deep inside my pockets, I was trying to protect myself against the cold and smeary April rain whilst I hurried along the pebble stone covered driveway. Finally I came to the house and ran through the large wooden double doors into the smart, professional and thankfully very dry reception area. I was greeted by the wonderful Mandy. All smiles she was not.

'Where have you been George? You're late, very late!' she scolded.

'Sorry Mandy, got caught up on a difficult repair job at the shop, old Jonesy wouldn't let me go.'

'Well it's the second time this week, you'd better get in there sharpish, they'll all be wanting their tea and you know how Sister gets if it's late?'

Dismissing me with a nod of her head, the gorgeous, untouchable blonde haired Mandy looked back down at her desk, picked up her nail file again and examined her long crimson nails closely. I hurried past her before she thought of anything else to criticise me about. And there would be plenty I thought, looking down at my tatty duffel coat, torn jeans and cheap plastic trainers. I sped around the corridor and into the staff wash room at the far end. I quickly slipped out of my damp coat and pulled on my purple work overall and barely had time to scrub my hands when I heard my name being called. I rushed out of the staff room and ran straight into the ample bosom of Sister Marion.

'Whoa there tiger,' she breathed in that superb husky voice of hers.

'Where are you going in such a rush?'

'Sorry Sister, I'm late, just couldn't get away from work,' I stammered.

'Don't worry,' Sister Marion said in that wonderful soothing voice of hers. 'The world's not going to end just because you're a few minutes late. You just get on and keep smiling. Oh and by the way, we have a new guest in Gaddesden Suite; she's a lovely old dear! Pop your head in and say hello will you?'

'OK will do Sister,' I called over my shoulder as I hurried off to the kitchen area.

By day I work in a TV repair shop on the high street, as an apprentice TV repair man to Mr Jones. Well, he calls me an apprentice, I think that's just so that he doesn't have to pay me very much. I spent three years at Salford University to earn my electrical engineering degree, and against the projections of all of my teachers I got a first. I wanted to be a radio frequency engineer - don't ask me why, it's just my thing. Yes, boring I know, but that's just me - you've been warned, don't let me corner you at a party. I haven't managed to get my dream job yet though, which is why I'm still working in a TV repair shop. I will get there one day though, I feel sure of it.

In the evenings I switch to my alter ego, where I work as a volunteer at our newly opened local hospice - the Hospice of St Francis, just off Shooters Way up in Northchurch village. I usually work about three hours an evening, serving teas, coffee and hot chocolate mainly, and doing a lot of washing up. Most weeks I'll work every evening, and sometimes I'll even come back on a Saturday or a Sunday if I'm doing nothing. What am I saying? I never do anything. All I normally have to look forward to is a lonely evening or weekend reading my radio magazines at home in my shabby little bedsit which is directly above the noisy betting shop in the high street. When things get really exciting I may also have a play around with my home built CB radio system, chatting to other sad radio obsessive loners like me. But don't think that's the only reason I volunteer at the hospice, no, far from it. I actually love it here. I especially love all the stories the old people have; the romances, the affairs, the heroic war stories, the non-heroic war stories, the gossip and the lives lived and loved. I really do plan to capture all of their stories and write a book one day. I'd so love to do that. I keep thinking I'd like to save up and buy one of those new dicta-phone things so I can record the stories and make sure that they're not lost forever. The problem is those things are so expensive and a little bit cumbersome to carry around. Maybe one day they'll be a bit cheaper and a bit smaller?

After loading my boiling hot water urn and all the other drinking paraphernalia onto my trolley, I started my evening's round. I looked in on old Mr Wreakspear in Boxmoor Suite first. Harry Wreakspear has cancer of the pancreas. He's been in now for about fourteen days and it's so noticeable how much he is deteriorating each day I see him. It's really such a shame. Old Harry is a real character. He was part of the second wave that went up the Normandy beaches on the 6th June 1944. A Sapper by trade, he's told me all about the bridges he built and destroyed, his mates who died, his mates who lived, his endless drinking sessions, and his dalliances with the local lasses in France and Germany. I recall he mentioned he even found time to have one or two brushes with 'Jerry'. How was anyone ever in any doubt that we would win the war with old soldiers like Harry on our side? He was indestructible. Well, he was back then, sadly though, not any longer. Harry was sleeping soundly so I quietly backed out of the room and made a mental note to pop back in again at the end of my round, after I'd seen to everyone else.

The next room was Gaddesden Suite, the one in which the new lady that Sister Marion had mentioned was occupying. Oh how I wish she would take me home and mother me with those fantastically great bosoms of hers - Sister Marion I mean! I eased into the room quietly, as I always do, just in case the patient is sleeping. Nope, she wasn't. The lady was sitting up in bed, looking very weak and with a distinct grey pallor to her wrinkled skin. She was propped up on her many pillows and reading a book. She had a full head of very long pure white hair and a striking pink knitted woollen shawl wrapped around her shoulders. Her 1960s style horn-rimmed glasses were also bright pink as was the lurid pink watch on her right wrist. I didn't get a good look but I think it was one of those new digital watches. I was liking her style very much, and I hadn't even spoken to her yet. She had obviously been quite a character in her time. Putting on my best smile I approached the bed, ready to take her drinks order. I don't think it was the look of absolute horror on her face when she looked up at me that stopped me dead in my tracks; I think it was more likely to be the large mud covered soldier sitting in the big armchair in the corner of the room that did it.

I didn't remember too much at the time, probably due to the shock, but later on I would recall vividly the khaki serge wool uniform, the black hobnail boots covered in dried mud, the puttees bound around the man's lower legs - partly covering his boots, and the jauntily-angled, somewhat bashed-in tin helmet perched on his head. Under the shadow of his tin helmet I remembered the man's very long and dark stubbly chin, his large bent hooked nose and his frighteningly dark, almost alien eyes looking intently at me. His hands were unusually white and with very long tapered fingers. The other thing I couldn't help but spot was the large rifle laying across his lap.

The old lady just sat there silently staring at me, her book gradually slipping from her hands, her jaw drooping down. I could see she was distraught so ignoring the armed man in the corner I moved closer to her to see if she was OK. As I approached the bed she reared backwards, dropping the book onto the floor and finally letting out what can only be described as a wolf-like howl. I looked again at the soldier, but he seemed not to be reacting, he was just sitting there looking at me curiously, and somewhat disconcertingly fiddling with the bolt of his rifle. Now it was my turn to stand, transfixed, not knowing what to do. Unfortunately my extensive electrical engineering university training hadn't provided me with any skills in dealing with this scenario. Mind you, I suspect that would have been the case for most people. It seemed to be forever that we were transfixed like that, staring at each other, our faces locked in terror. But in reality it was probably only a few seconds later when Sister Marion came running into the room accompanied by Helen, our newest staff nurse, the love of my life - if only she knew it. Sister Marion rushed straight up to the old lady, whom I later found out was called Violet. Helen stood directly in front of me and demanded to know what had happened. I couldn't fathom why neither of them had as yet noticed the soldier, who was worryingly now getting to his feet. Helen again asked me firmly what had happened whilst Sister Marion was trying to calm Violet down and get her to sip some water. I think I must have stammered something about the soldier in the corner with the gun because Helen gave me a very strange look and simply put both of her hands on my chest and forcibly pushed me backwards out of the room.

'George, why did Violet scream like that? What happened in there?' Helen demanded.

'I don't really know,' I responded. 'I think it must have been the soldier she saw.' But I knew in my heart of hearts it wasn't the soldier. She hadn't even been looking at the soldier when she had her shock and screamed - she had been looking directly at me.

'What are you talking about George? What soldier? Have you been drinking or taking drugs or something?'

'No of course not,' I responded timidly.

'I always knew you weren't right in the head George, but this is ridiculous.'

I had the distinct feeling that any chance I might have had with the delightful Helen was now rapidly slipping away from me. At that point Sister Marion - and her giant breasts - came bounding out of the room. She had the biggest smile ever on her face.

'George, Violet is soooo sorry,' Sister Marion beamed.

'Whaaa wha??' I stuttered.

'Violet, she's mortified. She says that it was just when you came in, you caused her the greatest shock ever.'

'Why?' I asked. I know I have that effect on most women that I try and chat to, but not usually those in their nineties.

'Violet says that you are the absolute double of her husband…well at least as he was when she last saw him.'

'What do you mean? I can't be, I'm only 24.'

'I know, apparently you are his exact double from the day when she kissed him goodbye on the platform, when he left to go to war. That was in 1915, and he never came back!'

'Oh,' was about all I could muster.

'Well come on, you need to go back in, Violet feels bad and she wants to apologise to you,' said Sister Marion as she dragged me back towards the room.

'But what about the soldier?' I said as I was being pushed and manhandled.

'Why does he keep going on about a bloody soldier?' I heard Sister Marion ask Helen, as she pushed me again towards the doorway.

'Dunno, if you ask me he's never been right in the head that lad, he needs help if you ask me,' Staff Nurse Helen said, dismissively.

'She's off my bloody Christmas card list,' I thought as I re-entered the room. There was Violet sitting up in bed, glasses off now, and I could see her eyes were red and still tear filled. And, there was the soldier, now standing on the other side of the bed looking straight at me. I noticed, with some relief, that he had left his rifle propped up against the chair in the corner.

'I'm so sorry if I startled you earlier Violet, ' I began.

'No, no, no, dear boy, it's all my fault, really it is. I am just being such a silly old woman that's all,' she said weakly. 'But you do look so like my husband. I know it's been nearly seventy years since I saw him last, but I haven't forgotten anything about him in all that time. I can even remember his hair, the way it always did its own thing - however much oil he put on it. I remember how he smelt. I remember how he used to feel when I put my arms around him. I even remember the fact that he'd forgotten to shave that morning in all the excitement. I can still remember everything about George, and you're his exact double I think.'

'George? That's my name too,' I blurted out without thinking.

I rushed over and grabbed Violet's hand just as I saw the tears welling up in her eyes again.

'Please Violet, let's not get upset again, how about a nice cup of tea?' I suggested.

'Yes, thank you…George…that would be really lovely,' she said, before coughing violently into a tissue.

I walked back over to my trolley and started making a cup of tea for the both of us. Helen came in again at that point and said that as it was quiet, Sister Marion had asked her to take my trolley and make the drinks for the remaining patients while I chatted to Violet. I have to say, she didn't look very impressed. Ah well, yet another potential girlfriend slipping from my grasp! I can't even remember the last girlfriend I had; I think it must have been bad-breath Becky from sixth form. As I think I may have mentioned before, I've not been altogether very successful with members of the fairer sex…or anything else much for that matter.

I was still in a quandary about the soldier. He had returned to his seat now but he was still watching me intently as he fiddled with his rifle again. Throughout the events of the past half hour no one had mentioned the soldier with the gun. No one, not a word, zilch. What could I make of that? Perhaps I was the only one seeing him? That was probably the only logical explanation I had. One other possible explanation was that maybe he was always around Violet and she knew he was there and consequently never mentioned him. Maybe, but on the other hand I wasn't going to strike up a conversation with her about the armed soldier in the corner of the room and risk having her screaming again. Besides, Helen already thought I was a sandwich short of a picnic and I wasn't about to make that even worse by starting up a conversation about ghosts. So, as hard as it was, I tried to ignore him. I reasoned with myself that I would give the 'ghost' - or whatever he was - a lot more thought later and try to come up with some feasible answers.

'Here's your tea Violet, I hope you like it strong?'

'Oh yes dear, I do, and two sugars too please if you would?'

Sitting down on the chair at Violet's bedside I had no problem striking up a conversation with her. It's funny how I am so relaxed with patients and can talk to them all night long with ease, even the female variety. But when I come to having to talk to a girl, like really talk to a girl, I just get the hot and cold sweats and clam up tight. Life's just not fair I thought.

'So Violet, would you mind telling me about George. if it's not too painful that is?'

'No my dear, I would love to tell you all about my darling George now, but where do I begin?'

'Well Violet, as they always say, why don't you begin at the beginning, let's start from when you met?'

So then Violet began to tell me the story of her younger life. Violet had been born to Sarah Walsh in the small Hertfordshire village of Great Berkhampsted on the 16th of February 1895. Sarah's parents ran a small greengrocer's shop on Berkhampsted high street, a business that had been in the family for many generations. Violet was born in the single bedroom of their flat directly over the small shop. Violet was Sarah's first child and was born out of wedlock - Sarah was only sixteen years of age at the time. As this was considered almost a crime back in those days, it was all covered up and Violet was brought up by Sarah's parents - her grandparents - as their child. As a result, she always thought of Sarah as her older sister rather than her mother. The family were extremely hard working and were considered to be reasonably affluent by the standards of the day. George first appeared on the scene when Violet was about sixteen. His family had moved into the village from Uxbridge, a small town west of London, about twenty miles away. George's father, William Puttnam, had secured a position as head blacksmith with W. Nash & Sons Blacksmiths - also located in the High Street - and he had relocated his whole family, including his wife and seven children away from the bustle of Uxbridge Town and into the relative peace of the Hertfordshire countryside. George was also sixteen at the time, the eldest of all his siblings, and he was employed by his father as a shoeing-smith, a specialist in the forging and fitting of horseshoes. Violet recalled how she and George used to promenade past each other's shops whenever they had the chance, and she was always dropping into the blacksmith's forge with a spare apple or pear or something for George and his dad.

'It was love at first sight my dear,' Violet leaned forward and whispered into my ear. 'I don't mind telling you I was struck by his amazing head of curly black hair, his deep hazel eyes and his handsome features right from the start. I loved the way his muscles flexed while he was hammering those white hot horseshoes over the anvil, I was a virgin then you know,' Violet confided.

'Too much information Violet,' I scolded her in a conspiratorial way. We both smiled.

'My parents, sorry - grandparents, weren't convinced at the start, but I managed to introduce them to William and Amy fairly soon after they had moved in and to my great relief they said that they approved of the Puttnam family. Those years were bliss I don't mind telling you young man. We were content to go the local theatre and even occasionally for walks across the common in the early summer evenings, but we couldn't touch back in those days. Not that I didn't want to mind,' Violet smiled at the delicious memory of it all.

'So what happened Violet, when did you marry George?'

'We married on Christmas day 1912, I wasn't quite 18 then. It might sound strange now but that was the only day in the year both our parents could take any time away from their work. It was a busy day, many young couples used to get married on Christmas Day for the same reasons. We had a lovely wedding and a bit of a shindig back at the old Highwayman public house for the family afterwards. Those were happy days George, so happy.'

Violet absolutely beamed across her whole face whilst she was recounting her wedding day story to me, yet her smile was also tinged with sadness as she remembered those happier times.

'Where did you live Violet and did you have any children?' I asked.

'Yes dear. George managed to secure a new job with old Mr Kempster at his blacksmith's premises which was over at Boat Inn Yard by the canal. Mr Kempster offered him a job as the senior shoeing smith and farrier. George's dad was really sorry to see him go but this was a wonderful opportunity for George and Mr Kempster had also offered us a small house next to the smithy at no 9 George Street to go with the job, as long as we looked after his business. That was just too good an opportunity to miss, so we jumped at the chance. Old Mr Kempster must have been in his seventies by then and he was really too tired to carry on much longer with his business. Unfortunately he didn't have any sons of his own to leave the business to and he kind of took George under his wing. It certainly was a wonderful time.' Violet smiled broadly again.

'So any children?' I pushed Violet gently.

Violet had a spasm of coughing before she could continue and I caught sight of some blood in the tissue she held in her hand. I had quite forgotten that she was extremely ill and so weak from the ravages of liver cancer. Her coughing fit sadly reminded me of the reality of her situation. She probably didn't really have much time left I thought, sadly.

'Ah yes, two beautiful girls,' Violet continued. 'Of course, George wanted a boy I feel sure, but he never let on even if he was disappointed. He doted on those girls you know. Evelyn was born on the 29th of November 1913 and baby Daisy came along on the 19th of February 1915. Of course, the war was on by then and we were all very worried, what with the zeppelin raids and all, but we were so much in love and we just believed in the future, our future. We never dreamed that it could all come to an end.'

'So what happened Violet, did it all come to an end?' I asked, but regretted asking that question immediately as I was loath to spoil her happy reminiscing.

Violet's face changed instantly as a deep sadness and melancholy settled over her.

'George felt he had to do his duty. All of his pals were volunteering for the front, the Kitchener posters were up everywhere and by 1915 some fellers were starting to receive white feathers. That was horrible George. The women were making things very difficult for the young men at that time and the emotional blackmail was too much for most men. George certainly didn't want to leave me and his babies, but we all knew he had to go. He was a fit young man and if he didn't go, I feel certain we wouldn't have been able to continue to live in the village afterwards. We talked about it day and night for months. We talked about it over breakfast in those early hours before George left to open up the smithy. We talked about it in the living room over a glass of stout during those long dark evenings while the girls were sound asleep upstairs in their cots. Finally we agreed, reluctantly, that he should go. We argued with ourselves that he would probably be called up anyway and while he had the chance he should volunteer to go into the Royal Field Artillery as a shoeing smith or a farrier so that he could look after the horses. We, perhaps naively, reasoned that at least that might not be too dangerous a job?'

'So when did he go Violet?' I asked, taking hold of her hand again and giving it a squeeze.

'I remember it as if it were yesterday. We walked together up to the recruiting office which was in the town hall. That was on the 29th March 1915, I'll never forget it. We had the girls with us but George got all embarrassed as we approached as there were crowds of men milling around outside. George asked me to take the girls home and he went inside, alone. I remember that I didn't go straight home. I went for a long walk around the common that afternoon, in a bit of a daze. I vaguely remember looking at the new tented village which had sprung up behind the station to house the Inns of Court Officers Training Corps who had been training there since late the previous year. On the common there were miles and miles of trenches dug which were supposed to resemble the trenches we had heard about on the western front. I didn't like the look of them much but they did at least look quite secure and reasonably dry and comfy. I remember thinking that I hoped George would be able to get posted to a nice dry and safe trench like those on the common. That was a laugh wasn't it? How naive I was back then. By the time I got home with the girls, George was already there with the kettle on and his signed enlistment papers on the table. I felt sick.'

'What happened then Violet?'

'I don't remember much of that time really George. I do remember we just held each other all of that night, and for many nights to come after that. George had to go and collect his uniform about ten days later and that was when I did really get upset. I think at that point, seeing him in his uniform, the realisation finally set in and I knew for certain he was going. Of course he still had many months of training to do before he went off to the front, and he was away for weeks at a time doing that. In between times George taught me the art of making a horseshoe and shoeing a horse. I didn't have the muscles but I was a fast learner and I had a good technique, even old Mr Kempster said so. By the time that George finally left for the front I could forge a reasonable horseshoe and re-shoe a horse. I could even repair a saddle or a bridle if necessary. George was very impressed with me. It was just as well, there were no other men left in the village who could have taken over. George was finally posted overseas on the 27th August 1915. That's a day I shall never forget. He was only twenty one years of age.'

'Please don't Violet, you don't have to relive that for me. It must be very painful?'

'My dear boy, don't worry I have relived that day every night for the past sixty nine years and I have cried many tears over it. Believe me, I remember every minute of that day, every smell, every colour, every word and every emotion. I don't get the chance to relive it with many people nowadays so don't worry, I'm happy to.'

Violet smiled genuinely, and her smile reached her eyes.

'OK if you are sure Violet,' I said as I squeezed her hand just a little harder.

'I remember everything was a rush that Friday morning. We had laid George's uniform and pack out the evening before and did our best to make sure we got up early. George had been accepted into the Royal Field Artillery and had to be in Woolwich barracks in west London by 5.00pm that afternoon. To do that he had to be on the 09.45 train leaving Berkhampsted station that morning. I was going with him and I had to get the girls ready in time as I was certainly not going to let him go without me. We managed to get everything done, had breakfast and we were out of the house by 09.00. It was just a short walk from our house in George Street over to the station. George paid for his ticket at the little ticket office and we walked onto the platform. I remember there were quite a few people on the station platform already, and a few of them were in uniform like George, saying their goodbyes to their loved ones. It was so very sad George, it really was. I just can't tell you how sad.'

I looked up at Violet as she wiped a tear away from her eye, using the delicate pink lace handkerchief she held in her hand.

'Of course baby Daisy was asleep in her pram and Evelyn didn't really understand what was going on. She knew from the way that her dad hugged her so tightly and the fact that I was crying that something was wrong, but George kept telling her that he would only be away for a short while and would bring her a lovely present back from France, so that made her very happy. George and I simply held each other tightly until the train pulled noisily into the station, surrounding us with hot billowing steam. We didn't want to let go of each other. Finally George managed to pull away and hauled himself up into one of the carriages. He closed the door behind him and we held hands for the last time through the open window. The conductor's whistle shrilled out, and with another woooosh of steam, the train started to move away, taking my George with it, to the front, into danger. I don't know how long I stood there waving, long after the train had disappeared from sight I think. I remember slowly turning and walking away from the station, holding Evelyn's hand and pushing the big coach built pram we had. I think I must have been numb, I don't remember much of the rest of that day if I'm honest.'

Just as Violet raised her hanky again to wipe the now more freely flowing tears from her eyes, the door to the room opened gingerly and two elderly ladies with the biggest smiles on their faces stepped into the room.

'Hello Mum!' they both seemed to shout in unison.

Getting up from my chair, I managed to let go of Violet's hand and with some embarrassment, I wiped my own tears away on my sleeve before I looked up to greet the newcomers.

'Hello girls,' Violet was beaming ear to ear. 'Meet my new friend George; he's the double of your Dad.'

The two ladies were so obviously sisters. Both had pure white hair like their mum and were about the same height. They were both very well turned out in smart skirt suits, one brown and one blue, with matching handbags and surprisingly enough, high heeled shoes. I'd say they looked to be in their sixties, and very sprightly with it. I thought all old ladies wore 'comfortable' flat shoes and frumpy old cardigans at that age. Not these two, they were quite elegant.

'Evelyn and Daisy I presume?' I ventured.

'Yes, right first time, I'm Evelyn, it's nice to meet you,' said the lady in the blue suit. 'I'm guessing mother has been boring you with all of her tales?'

'No, not at all, she's a wonderful and very interesting lady,' I said as I sidestepped around the two ladies and backed up towards the door. I risked a glance to my right and sure enough the soldier was still sitting there, watching the proceedings intently. I had been so engrossed in Violet's story that I had actually forgotten about him. I looked back at the two ladies approaching their mother's bed and it was obvious they had not seen the soldier either. I rubbed my eyes and stared harder at him this time, but he was still there, large as life - if indeed he was alive, although somehow I suspected not.

Violet and her two daughters were looking at me strangely as I bumbled backwards out of the door, mumbling something incomprehensible about coming back later to pick up the cups. I snatched one last glance at the strange soldier, who was still sitting there with those dark eyes staring straight into mine, I stepped out of the door and closed it quietly behind me.

'Phew!'

Still in a bit of a daze I went and found Nurse Helen, who was now back in the kitchen refilling the urn with boiling water.

'I'll take over again now Helen,' I offered in the huskiest voice I could muster up.

Helen just looked at me once with the most dismissive eyes she could muster and then brushed past me out of the kitchen, without saying a word. I spent the next hour and a half finishing off the drinks and biscuit round, making sure I looked in on Mr Wreakspear again at the end. Finding him awake I made him his usual hot chocolate with two Garibaldi biscuits, his favourites. I collected all of the cups again, but carefully avoided Violet's room, partly because I didn't want to disturb her valuable time with her daughters and partly because I didn't want to face that soldier ghost - or whatever he was - again. I stopped and had my usual five minute flirt with Sister Marion before I left for the evening, and as usual, got nowhere. Then, pulling on my old duffel coat, I walked out past the empty reception desk and stepped back out into the rain filled night.

Hurrying along Shootersway and turning left down into Durrants Lane on my way back to the high street, I kept thinking about the soldier. I was beginning to recall his features in some detail now, the fact that he was unusually tall, that strange awkward gangly look he had, that striking crooked nose and those dark, dark eyes in particular. Nothing about him seemed ghost like, he seemed as real as anyone else. Yet it was obvious no one else could see him. At least I think that was the case. Who was he? Was he attached in some way to Violet? Did he have anything to do with the death of her husband in the First World War? I wasn't too clued up on uniforms of the British Army, past and present, but it did seem to me that it could have been a uniform of a Tommy from that war. In which case, I could see there being some kind of link to her husband, George. And what of that? Why was Violet so convinced at first sight that I was actually George, her husband from 1918? Was that just a coincidence? Somehow I didn't think so. The way the soldier's eyes never left me added weight to that. He wasn't staring at Violet or her daughters when they came in, I knew he was only staring at me. I've never really believed in coincidences, and this was a whole string of them that were ringing a whole load of alarm bells in my head.

I dropped into the chippy three doors down from my flat and got myself a chicken pie and chips. It wasn't the best food in the world but it was hot and occasionally edible. Besides, I liked to chat with Mary, the lady who managed the fish shop. She was a large rotund lady who was always smiling and cheerful. I suspected she was a lot younger than she looked and she was always flirting with me, but strangely enough I still felt comfortable with her and was able to flirt back. After the usual jesting around, I left the shop, shielding my hot package from the rain. I soon came to the entrance to my flat, which was next to the betting shop doorway. Kicking open the broken wooden side gate I hurried down the dark alleyway and round to the steel staircase at the rear of the shop. I climbed the wet stairs two at a time and leaned up against the door to my modest, no sorry - let's be honest here, decrepit little flat, fumbling in my pocket for the single Yale key.

Once inside, I hung up my wet coat on the old Victorian coat stand in the tiny hallway, took off my trainers and went through the single door to my lounge and kitchenette. I flicked on the one piece of modern technology that I possessed - my new blue Sanyo music centre - and the radio hummed into life, blaring out Adam Ant's latest hit - *Goody Two Shoes*. I pulled a can of Tenants strong lager from the fridge and sat down on one of my two comfy old leather armchairs, the only furniture I had in the room. My head was still reeling with the events of the evening. It felt like something out of a fantasy novel or a ghost story and it was certainly giving me the creeps. The first can of beer went down quickly and I could feel the effects of the 9% alcohol lager soothing my chaotic mind. The blue cans were on special at the local off-license so I thought I'd give them a go. I felt sure it was the same stuff the down and outs drank in the park. Anyway, it tasted OK and seemed to be doing the job.

After finishing off my pie and chips and the second can of beer I started to feel a bit mellower about the whole soldier thing and convinced myself that maybe it was just a ghost I saw, and it was probably the ghost of George - Violet's husband - just hanging around her? If I'd have thought a bit harder I would have remembered that the ghost looked nothing like me and had the appearance of being quite a bit older, maybe in his late forties - assuming of course ghosts have ages - so would almost certainly not be George.

House of Fun by Madness blared on the radio as I closed my eyes, suddenly overcome with tiredness and most likely, alcohol. I couldn't be bothered to get up and go to bed or even to switch the radio off. The last thing I remembered before I drifted off were those dark eyes peering out from under that battered tin helmet.

I think it was probably the waft of smoke that awoke me. I could taste it and it was stinging the back of my throat. I started to cough. Dazed, I first opened one eye and then the other. Trying to collect my thoughts and with a rising sense of panic I wondered if perhaps the flat was on fire, but no, that was definitely smoke from a cigarette, not a fire, which made no sense at all. Was I still dreaming perhaps? With my thoughts slowly coming together into some order as I woke myself up a bit more, I realised that I was still sitting in my armchair. I had no idea how long I had been asleep, but it must have been at least an hour or two. The streetlights cast a dull glow around the curtained window but the room was pretty much in darkness, so it was obviously still sometime in the middle of the night. With my heart hammering I sat there very still, sniffing the air. The cigarette smoke was overpowering now that I was awake. No wonder I had been coughing in my sleep. I also noticed the strange silence; the radio had been turned off. I knew it had been on when I dozed off. My eyes were finally starting to adjust but I still couldn't see very much in the gloom. With a real sense of foreboding I sensed more than saw that there was someone sitting in the armchair on the other side of the room, someone looking at me. Without moving I stared harder into the blackness and just then I saw the embers of a cigarette light up. A cold shiver ran up and down my spine and I thought I was going to faint with terror.

'Come on, get a grip,' I whispered to myself under my breath, and took a few deep breaths in an attempt at calming myself down. I breathed in another waft of cigarette smoke and remembered thinking that it actually smelled quite soft and pleasantly aromatic, not like the usual clouds of acrid smoke you get when standing in a pub. It was more like the smell of pipe tobacco. Having successfully analysed the smoke I finally began to wonder why someone might be in my flat in the middle of the night, smoking a cigarette. I should have been up and running around screaming at this point, or at least running for the door, but I felt strangely calm. I knew it was the soldier.

'Why are you here?' I asked calmly.

The cigarette lit up again and another waft of smoke drifted over me. I wasn't at all sure that ghosts could even speak so I jumped when an answer came.

'We've been waiting for you son. I knew you'd turn up eventually,' was all he said. His voice was deep and gravelly, probably as a result of all the cigarettes I thought. Do ghosts really smoke? I wondered.

'What do you want?' I ventured again.

It seemed like an age before he answered.

'You have unfinished business son, you have to go back. A lot depends upon it, more than you could possibly imagine.'

This conversation was becoming stranger by the minute. The soldier was very unnerving, but he didn't sound too threatening. I pinched myself to make sure I was actually awake and not dreaming all of this. It definitely seemed that indeed, unfortunately I was very much awake.

'What unfinished business? Go back where? I've never met you before, I think you've got the wrong person,' I blurted out, rather more shakily now.

The soldier paused again before answering.

'It would take too long to explain George, it's very complex, but we have to go now, right now. Violet is slipping away and time is running out. You just need to know that it's very very important and that you have to try harder this time, you can't give up like last time, you have to fight. Fight for your life and survive, you mustn't give up, you must get back home.'

'I am home, I don't know what the hell you're talking about,' I stammered.

'I know George,' the soldier said softly, in an almost empathetic manner. 'If I tried to explain you'd never believe me so I think it's best if we just do this and get it over with. You must remember what I say though, whatever happens, whatever struggles you face, you must fight and you must succeed. You have to go home. Just remember that and you have to watch out for yourself. I will be with you and will help where I can; you are not on your own.'

At that point I began thinking that this soldier was obviously some escaped demented crazy who was spouting a complete load of old bollocks. I was just about to get up and switch on the light when the soldier made his move. He lifted his tall gangly frame out of his chair and stepped across to me in one fluid, graceful movement which belied his apparent awkwardness. I more sensed it that saw it and I almost jumped out of my skin when he laid his large hand on my right shoulder. It wasn't a threatening touch, more of a fatherly gesture. I then had that awful sinking sensation you sometimes get in the lower part of your stomach when you know something bad is about to happen. He laid his other hand on my left shoulder as he drew his face closer and looked me intently in the eyes. Staring at his unnaturally bright blue eyes I remember thinking, he doesn't feel like a ghost, I could even smell his tobacco laden breath on my face, and was that a trace of whisky too?

Calmly he then said 'let's go George, time's running out.'

And with just a hint of that strange fizzing feeling you get when you have an anaesthetic, everything went black.

Chapter Three

Bapaume, France - 23 March 1918

I awoke in darkness, underwater and with someone holding me down. 'Terror' just doesn't do justice to my state of mind at that point. My mind was still reeling with trying to work out what had happened since the soldier put his hands on my shoulders back in the flat, looked into my eyes, and now suddenly I was outside in the cold and having to cope with drowning. I pushed up and tried to kick out at the same time and all I got for my trouble was an agonising pain shooting right down my right leg. I almost passed out again with the agony and my face was still underwater. I was gasping to take a breath and my head was beginning to swim. I could feel a dead weight across my back and shoulders and it was pushing me further down, under the water. I was now beginning to panic - big time. I could feel that the whole top half of my body was being held under water and my lungs were screaming for me to take a breath. My mind was telling me not to, and I think my lungs were just about to win that argument when I remembered the soldier's words, 'you must fight, you must try harder, and don't give in'. Was this what he meant? With renewed energy I pushed my hands down. I wasn't floating; I appeared to be lying in shallow water. My hands sank into what seemed like squidgy thick mud underneath me. I pushed down again with as much energy as I could gather and tried to lift my head and shoulders above the water, straining my neck and shoulder muscles to the point of tearing. I left the lower part of my body where it was in the mud, like a big press-up. I managed to shift the weight from my back a little, so I pushed again, harder this time. The burning pain in my neck, shoulders and lungs was incredible but it didn't even begin to compare with the pain shooting down my right leg which was just unbearable.

I managed to lift my head clear of the water, just for a second or two, but it was enough to take a gasp of air before I fell back under the weight again. With the soldier's words 'you must fight' still ringing in my ears I tried again for a fourth time. This time, with immense relief the weight on my back suddenly slipped away and I was able to lift myself up out of the water. The problem now was that the mud below me was beginning to suck my hands and wrists downwards. I had to get out of this hole or whatever it was, and quickly. The weight that had been on my back had fortunately now slipped completely off to my left. I looked around and saw that it was a body, another soldier. He was now just lying there with his face in the mud and water. With my remaining strength I forced myself over to the left and screaming out in pain as I did so, I used his body as a solid base over which to roll myself. I was now laying on my back in mud on the other side of the soldier, panting hard, but thankfully now above the water line. I laid there trying to ease the pain in my leg and get my breath back again. Suddenly remembering the soldier I reached over again and with my left hand and I grabbed the hair on his head and pulled his face clear of the water. I had no idea whether he was alive or not and whether he had in fact been trying to kill me, in which case it was possibly the silliest thing in the world to try and pull him out of the water, but anyway, I guess it's still a basic human instinct to save another life if you can. As I pulled his head up he groaned and gasped for breath, so with all my remaining strength I pulled him around onto his side so that at least he was now lying with his face above the water.

I have no idea how long I laid there like that. I didn't want to move because of the pain so I tried to keep still and take in my surroundings. It was dark and the sky was cloudless. There were more stars out than I can ever remember seeing and the sky was absolutely amazing. The stars looked normal and I could even make out the shape of the Plough above me, which was just about the only constellation I was ever able to recognise. Seeing the Plough made me feel a little more comfortable somehow. I wasn't sure where I was but at least I was still on the same planet. That helped. Looking around me all I could really see in the darkness was a wall of thick wet mud. It was obvious that I was laying in some kind of a large muddy hole with a fairly deep pool of water at the bottom. I looked down at myself and saw that I too now was wearing a dark brown uniform; a soldier's uniform, like the one the ghostly soldier had been wearing. I was no expert but I knew this was an old fashioned uniform type, like the ones used in the last two world wars. It was hard to see in the dark but the guy next to me seemed to be wearing a similar type uniform but it looked to be more of a dark green, certainly a different shade to mine. He was lying on his side and away from me and I couldn't see any badges or insignia or anything so I had no idea whether we were on the same side or not, but just based on the colour of uniform I had to assume we probably weren't. I looked around our hole again and in the darkness I could just about make out that the mud wasn't at all smooth. There were bits and pieces of wood, twisted metal and wire sticking out of the mud everywhere. As my eyes adjusted, I could also make out other things half buried in the mud that I didn't even want to guess what they were, but which looked suspiciously like body parts. My mind was certainly in denial on this, but from all of the pictures and films I had ever seen I would have to think that this looked very much like a scene from the First World War, and I was lying in the bottom of a shell hole in no-man's-land.

It was then that I heard a high pitched squealing sound way overhead followed by a terrific 'crump' sound which shook the mud I was laying on violently. A whole load of mud and debris then rained down on me as I covered my head with my arms.

'Bloody hell!' I shouted out. 'This is a sodding nightmare!'

That confirmed it for me then. As mind boggling as it was, somehow, either in mind or body, or both, I had been transported back to what seemed like the western front at some point in world war one. It's strange how the mind copes in situations like these. I knew it just wasn't possible that I could have been in my flat in 1984 one minute, and then miraculously transported back to world war one in the next. But unless this was some kind of ultra-real dream or hallucination, all of my senses were telling me that was exactly where I now was. I suppose it must be a kind of natural reaction to shock or some other very basic instinctive survival mode that kicks in to keep you alive, and sane, but I wasn't laying there denying any of this was actually happening - as I should have been - I seemed to be already quite accepting of the new situation I was in and was now trying to think of a way to get out of it. Funny creatures we humans!

I tried to move again but the pain in my leg was absolutely horrendous. It burned deeply throughout my whole right side and made me feel quite nauseous. I thought immediately of one of those children's pain charts you see on the wall in the accident and emergency department at the local hospital. If I had to choose, I would definitely pick the one with the sad face and the tear in the eye at that moment. Just then another high pitched whistle came from overhead. This time I tensed up and waited for the inevitable loud crump of the shell exploding and the shuddering of the earth beneath me. The guy next to me moaned again and started to roll over. I thought to myself, if he's unfriendly, I'm done for. He rolled right over then and faced me in the mud, his nose about six inches away from mine. We lay there for what seemed like ages just staring at each other. The same thoughts obviously running through his mind as they were mine. I could almost hear the cogs in his mind whirring around. Finally his eyes seemed to clear and rather abruptly he sat up and moved a little way away from me. Looking up at him I could now see that his uniform was in fact a dull green woollen material and he had black leather shoulder straps, belt and ammo pouches. He didn't have a helmet on but I could see he had a severe short-back-and-sides haircut with a long mop of curly blond hair on top. He had a fairly rugged, unshaven and muddy face but I thought, hoped maybe, that his blue eyes had a kindly look about them. From all of the pictures I'd seen I would definitely put my money on him being a German.

The German soldier looked me up and down, obviously taking in the fact that I wasn't going to be leaping up and attacking him any time soon.

His first words to me were simply 'Danke.'

Then he quickly moved away from me and crept up the side of the muddy hole we were in to peer over the top. He took some time looking carefully in all directions before he slid back down the mud, next to me.

'You English?' He asked.

Somewhat surprised by his use of English I confirmed that I was indeed English.

'Thank you,' he said again, this time in English.

'For what?' I asked.

'For lifting me from the water, I would have drowned otherwise.'

'Ah yes,' I responded, thinking it was perhaps an act of over generosity on my part, especially as he had just tried to drown me. I then noticed the nasty wound to the left side of his head, which was bleeding quite freely. He instinctively raised his fingers to the wound and touched it gingerly, immediately wincing in pain.

'You are wounded also,' he said, pointing down at my leg.

'Am I?' I asked, somewhat stupidly. I obviously was, but I had no idea as to how or when.

'What is your name?' He asked.

'George, and yours?' I said.

'Karl,' he responded and to my great surprise he reached over and offered his hand. I shook his hand and then he seemed to relax a little and sat back down in the mud, but still looking at me intently.

'Where are we?' I asked.

Karl's face immediately lit up in a huge grin.

'Who knows?' He said. 'Somewhere in a big hole of mud I think.'

I joined him in his little joke and laughed too.

'So,' he said. 'We need to get out of here before one of those shells drops in here with us, or one of our sides decides to start another attack.'

'I guess so,' I responded, fully expecting my new buddy to clamber back up the side of the hole and disappear over the top, back to wherever he came from.

'I think we need to do something about your leg before we move you though,' he said, looking around the hole.

'Why, am I coming with you?' I asked, adding as an afterthought 'am I your prisoner?'

The German looked at me again and laughed loudly.

'My prisoner? Why would I want to take you as my prisoner? No, I am your prisoner Englander.' He laughed heartily again. 'You will take me back to your lines as your prisoner I think.'

'OK, that's fine with me, I'll need a hand though, and I don't even know where my lines are,' I said, smiling at this bizarre situation.

With that, Karl the German started to search around the hole again. Finally he picked up a rifle which was lying next to us. He wiped as much mud off it as he could against his trouser leg and then he removed the ammunition clip from underneath and pulled open the bolt, making sure there were no bullets in the breech. He then brought the rifle over to my right leg. He drew out a large bayonet from his belt, which startled me somewhat for a moment, and then proceeded to cut through the puttee which was bound tightly around the bottom of my leg and removed it. Ignoring my obvious discomfort he placed the rifle against my leg, binding the puttee tightly around both the stock and my leg, forming a makeshift splint. When he had finished he sat back again surveying his work.

'Ja, that should do nicely for now George,' he said seriously.

Just then another shell exploded nearby, showering us both in debris, and we could hear the not too distant rattle of machine guns.

'We need to go now I think,' the German said.

Thus began my epic journey back to what I hoped were the British lines and some kind of medical attention. All thoughts of how I had actually come to be in this war and in this situation had gone from my mind for the moment. As I said before, I think an instinctive survival mode kicks in somehow when you most need it. Your body and mind doesn't need to be distracted with analysing trivia such as - how did all this happen? I was certainly lucky to have found a 'friendly' German who for some reason also badly wanted to get safety over to the British lines. Perhaps he had just had enough of fighting, I wasn't sure and I wouldn't blame him, but I was very grateful for the help at that moment in time.

Karl grabbed the front of my tunic and literally dragged me up the side of the shell hole, through the mud. I wanted to scream with the pain coming from my leg, but I somehow managed not to. Biting down hard on the knuckles of my right hand helped a bit. Once at the top, Karl crawled over, turned around and dragged me over the top too, so we were both laying side by side out in the open. Having left the relative safety of the shell hole I suddenly felt very exposed lying out there in no-man's-land. However, all seemed relatively quiet and no shells had come near us for a while, so maybe we were going to be lucky. I had to hope so.

Having my first chance to look around, I noticed the night was black, really pitch black - about as black as a soldier's bloody future out here in no-man's-land I thought. Mind you, the darkness was probably a blessing too. As my eyes adjusted, I could just make out in the darkness a flat churned up landscape of mud with no other real features other than the occasional roll of coiled up barbwire. I had no idea which direction we needed to be going in, I hoped Karl did.

Karl was on his knees now, peering around intently.

'I don't think it will be far, the problem is making sure we're going in the right direction,' Karl whispered, almost to himself.

'OK, I think it's this way George,' he said, pointing with his hand in the general direction to our right.

'But we will need to crawl, I don't think it will be safe enough for us to walk, certainly not with your leg. Do you think you can manage that?' He asked.

'Yes,' I responded, more positively than I felt.

'OK let's go then, I'll lead, you follow. If you need to rest, let me know, but please just whisper. Voices carry a long way out here and we don't want to attract anyone's attention. Your snipers are good and the gunnery boys could certainly make a mess of us, so stay low and quiet. I'm not sure I trust my side either.'

I wasn't at all sure what Karl meant by his last comment. He then crawled off slowly in the direction he had just indicated. Using what strength I had left, I started to haul myself along using my hands, elbows and my good left leg. The pain was indescribable from dragging my right leg across the rough muddy ground but I knew it was the only way. No one was coming for me in an ambulance, so I had to do this if I was going to survive. I started to wonder what the hell had happened to my leg. I hadn't really managed to have a close look when we were back in the shell hole so I had no real idea what damage was there. I also had no idea how I had been hurt so badly. In my mind I had simply just arrived in that muddy water filled hole as soon as the soldier in my room touched my shoulders. There seemed to have been no time in-between. Everything about my last hour or so was undeniably bizarre and outside of any normality I could comprehend at this moment in time, so I reasoned it was probably better to stop thinking and to simply concentrate on crawling through the soft sticky mud for now. I had no idea what I was grabbing onto in the darkness. My hands were sinking down into the freezing cold black mud and I could feel bits of wood, rocks, pieces of twisted metal which cut into my hands and occasionally softer squishy lumps, which may have been parts of animals or humans, I had no way of knowing. The stench of decaying flesh and another acrid smell, something like sulphur, was all around me. The mud itself seemed to smell of death and decay. It was the stuff of nightmares.

'Karl! I need to rest up for a minute,' I whispered as loudly as I dared, after we had been crawling for what seemed like half an hour or so. My hands were coated in thick freezing mud and I could no longer feel my fingers. I was starting to worry about frostbite.

Karl stopped, turned to look at me and then crawled backwards to lay alongside me.

'I think we're nearly there George,' he whispered. 'I can hear voices just over there, in front of us, English voices I think.'

Just then there was a loud bang and a bright red flare shot up into the night sky just behind us.

'Down!' whispered Karl as we both flattened ourselves against the mud as best we could. Karl looked over at me.

'Keep your eyes closed George, otherwise your night vision will be ruined, and for God's sake don't move a muscle,' warned Karl. I hadn't thought of that, bloody greenhorn that I was.

As we lay there completely still, waiting for the bright red light to fade, I wondered about Karl. Who he was and how he came to be here?

'How come your English is so good Karl?' I asked.

'Ahh! My mother, she was English, she came from a nice little village called Princes Risborough in Buckinghamshire. We lived as a family in Göttingen, in Saxony. My father was a professor at the university there, and my mother she taught also. I always spoke English at home with my mother. My father encouraged that too, he said I would do well to be fluent in English. I think maybe he was right ja?'

'Yes, I think maybe it has come in quite handy now Karl,' I agreed. Handy for me anyway.

Just then we heard the chut-chut-chut-chut of a German machine gun opening up. This time it sounded a bit closer to us so I instinctively pushed my face down hard into the mud, closed my eyes tightly shut and tensed up my whole body. I had read somewhere that by the time you have heard the sound of a gun firing the bullet will already be half a mile past, so I'm not sure it was completely necessary, but when I looked I noticed that Karl had his head down too so I didn't feel too embarrassed. Then suddenly there was a long stream of what I can only describe as loud humming whistling sounds which sounded like a swarm of very fast and very angry bees buzzing over us, just inches above our heads. A moment later there was the chut-chut-chut-chut sound of the machine gun again. Phew, I'm glad I didn't have my head up that time, as I knew I wouldn't have one any longer. We waited for a few moments and then crawled on slowly again through the agonising black mud. From then on I was constantly waiting for the impact of a storm of bullets to tear into me, knowing now that they would arrive in silence, there would be no warning. The fear and the stress alone was almost totally incapacitating. I was trying desperately to control my breathing and I didn't know just how much longer I could keep this up. My nerves were going. A little while later Karl stopped and indicated for me to crawl up alongside him.

'George, when we reach the English trenches we will be challenged. You will have to do all the talking and tell them clearly who you are. You know, tell them your name, rank, unit and number and all that kind of stuff. And you will need to tell them you have a German prisoner with you. They will be very, how you say, jumpy, and we don't want them shooting both of us do we?'

The realisation dawned on me.

'Karl, I don't know any of that information. I mean, I know who I am of course, but I don't know what my rank is or any of that regimental stuff.'

'George, how can you not know that? You must know your rank and number, you are a soldier, you must,' Karl pleaded.

'Karl, I can't explain now, I just don't know it.'

'Maybe you had a blow to the head as well, a bit of concussion maybe?' Karl asked.

'Maybe,' I said. It was as good an excuse as any I thought, and one that I may be using quite a lot from here on in.

'Here, let me,' said Karl as he reached over to my throat and pulled out the cord that was around my neck. On the cord were two thin discs, one round and one octagonal. There seemed to be details stamped onto the discs.

'Let me look closer,' said Karl as he pulled one of the discs right up to his eye.

'The best I can make out is: G. Puttnam. RFA. Number 99243. C of E,' he said.

'Puttnam?' I asked.

'Well, that's your name isn't it?' asked Karl.

'Er, yes, it must be I suppose, of course it is,' I said, unconvincingly.

'C of E, that's Church of England. What's RFA?' I asked again.

'Well I'm not too familiar with British dog tags, but that must be your regiment, I think that stands for Royal Field Artillery. You had better memorise that number before we get to the British lines as every soldier knows his name, number and rank off by heart, and if you don't, we'll end up with a bullet between our eyes. Oh, and by the way, just in case you had forgotten that too, judging by the stripes on your arms you are a corporal.'

I looked down at my right arm and indeed there were two stripes sewn onto my tunic.

'OK got it, Corporal George Puttnam, number 99243 of the Royal Field Artillery,' I whispered out loud, and then continued to repeat over and over again in my head.

'OK let's move on,' Karl said. 'As soon as someone challenges us, you had better be ready with the answer.' He stared at me in the darkness with a grim face.

'OK, I will,' I tried to reassure him.

We crawled onwards again and sure enough I could also hear the voices, directly in front of us and what seemed like only feet away. Karl was right though, voices definitely do travel a long way across the stillness of no-man's-land as we must have crawled for at least another twenty minutes before we got to a slight rise in the earth and came up to a whole load of razor sharp coiled up barbwire. The voices were on the other side of what was obviously a trench parapet. Karl crawled back a little behind me, nudging me in my side. OK, so this was it. I looked around and noticed an almost straight line of soldiers laying in the semi darkness away to my right. They were all laying in varying grotesque positions in the mud. Obviously long dead and probably part of a previous attack from this trench. They had most likely been cut down by a deadly machine gun just as they stepped over the top. All of them sons or fathers, brothers or lovers. I wondered if their families knew yet or if they were still waiting, longing for them to come home. That sight hit me hard, it was such a surreal and depressing sight.

As we lay there, the sun was just appearing on the horizon directly behind us and daylight was slowly creeping up, illuminating our miserable world of mud. The landscape now took on an eerie red glow. I certainly felt like I had fallen into hell.

'Pssst, guys, is anyone there?' I whispered, loudly.

The voices in the trench stopped immediately.

'Is anyone there?' I whispered loudly again. 'My name's George Puttnam, Corporal George Puttnam and I need help.'

'Say your name, rank and number clearly again lad,' came a voice from the trench.

'It's George, Corporal George Puttnam, number 99243. I need help, I'm wounded,' I pleaded.

'What's your regiment lad?' came the voice again.

'I'm with the Royal Field Artillery.'

'When were you wounded?'

'I don't know,' I replied, honestly. 'I think it was yesterday or sometime during the evening, I'm a bit dazed. I've been in a shell hole for hours and have just managed to crawl here.'

'OK lad, I'm cutting a hole in the wire just in front of you, you'll have to crawl through.'

And with that, a tin helmet appeared over the top of the parapet, followed by two hands. The soldier started to cut the wire in front of him using a large pair of wire cutters. Fortunately he had big heavy gloves on so once he had made the necessary cuts he was able to push the wire apart just enough to allow a man to crawl through. As soon as he had finished his head disappeared. I took that as a sign to move ahead, so I crawled carefully through the gap, snagging my uniform on both sides as I went. As I reached the edge, I looked over and there were at least five soldiers standing below me in the trench, all with their rifles pointed directly at me. I tried to look relaxed and smile at them.

I eased myself over the edge and the biggest of the men shouted loudly 'ere, you two 'elp 'im down then.'

Two of the soldiers leaned their rifles against the trench wall and lifted their arms up to help me down. It was only as I was being carefully laid down into the trench that I remembered something important.

'Er, I've also got a German prisoner with me, he's right behind.'

They immediately dropped me into the bottom of the trench where I crumpled awkwardly into a moaning mess. The two who were helping me went for their rifles again. The big man, who I now noticed had three sergeants stripes on his arms, stepped forward to the front of the trench and shoved his rifle through the hole in the barbed wire.

'What did you say lad, is there someone else out there?'

'Yes, it's a German prisoner. He helped me get back here and he's unarmed, don't shoot him.'

'Kommen hier, handy hooch,' said the big sergeant in really bad German.

'He can speak good English,' I said.

'OK, get down here Fritz, and don't try anything,' the sergeant shouted again.

Karl's face then appeared over the edge of the trench. He looked scared, naturally, but he attempted a smile and then he managed to slide over the edge of the trench and tumble down, almost on top of me. No helping hands were offered this time. The soldiers all just pointed their rifles at the new arrival.

'Thomson, mend that bloody wire will ya, and quick about it,' ordered the sergeant.

The sergeant looked at the pair of us lying in the bottom of the trench.

'Peters, get a medic and a stretcher here, pronto. You, German, put your hands on your head. What's your name and regiment?'

Karl looked carefully at the sergeant and did as he was ordered.

'Unteroffizier Karl Von Ohain, Jäger Division, I am your obedient prisoner sir!' Karl responded as meekly as he could.

'Stand up Unteroffizier Karl Von Ohain,' said the sergeant.

Karl stood up slowly, keeping his hands away from his body and slightly raised, trying not to make anyone jumpy. Once he was upright he placed them back on his head again. It was only then that I realised just how tall Karl was. He towered head and shoulders above everyone else standing in the trench, including the sergeant. He also looked like he had the physique of a boxer or a weight lifter, with a huge chest, thick arms and an even thicker neck. The soldiers were understandably nervous of him.

'Do you have any weapons on you?' demanded the sergeant.

'Yes sir, but just my bayonet.'

'Rodgers, take the prisoner's bayonet will you?'

A soldier stepped forward and removed Karl's bayonet from its leather scabbard on his belt.

'Do you have any cigarettes on you?' asked the sergeant again.

'Yes sir, just a few,' responded Karl.

'Hand them over,' ordered the sergeant.

Karl carefully reached into his tunic top pocket with one hand and removed a small white packet with black print on it and handed it over to the sergeant. The sergeant took the packet and removed two cigarettes. He put both in his mouth whilst taking out a box of matches from his pocket with Lucifers clearly emblazoned on the front. He then struck a match and lit both cigarettes. He dragged the smoke deep down into his lungs, coughed up some phlegm, spat it over the top of the trench, then leaned over and handed one of the cigarettes to me.

'Ere, take this, it'll do you some good,' said the sergeant with what I almost detected to be a little bit of compassion.

I was just about to politely refuse and tell the sergeant that I didn't smoke, when thankfully, something stopped me. I took the cigarette from him and gingerly put it to my lips. The last time I had tried a cigarette was at the school disco, when I was about fourteen. It was horrendous and extremely embarrassing as I didn't stop coughing for about twenty minutes. Oh how they all laughed. I hoped that now I was grown up things might be different.

I took a drag of the cigarette and started to cough. Nope, still the same. I let out two coughs and managed to suppress the rest. My chest was on fire and my eyes were watering. I'd better get used to this I thought.

'OK you two,' the sergeant pointed to two of the soldiers. 'Take this German and get him over to the Lieutenant's dug out will yer. Do it quickly and make sure he doesn't try any funny business. If he does, shoot 'im.'

Karl looked down at me.

'Thank you my friend, until we meet again?'

'Thank you too,' I said. 'Take good care of yourself.' And I meant it.

Karl gave me a nod of his head and he smiled before turning and walking way up the trench with his hands on his head and one soldier in front and the other soldier behind him. I couldn't have foreseen it then, but I was going to be meeting Karl again in the not too distant future.

'So lad,' the sergeant said as he sat down on the wooden duckboards in the bottom of the trench, next to me. 'Tell me what happened out there?'

'Well I'm not totally sure sergeant. I must have been shot or something as all I remember was waking up in the bottom of a shell hole full of water.'

I then recounted my tale from the moment I came to consciousness under the water, and obviously leaving out anything to do with the strange events in my flat back in 1984. The sergeant looked down at my leg. With the daylight just beginning to come up I could now see the mess of torn fabric, congealed dried blood, torn flesh and something white, was that bone? Uggggh - I turned away. I've always been squeamish as far as blood and gore were concerned, especially my own.

'You're very lucky lad. You must have been out there since yesterday's fighting. That's a nasty one lad right enough, but as I said, you're lucky, it looks like a gunshot wound to your knee. Pretty clean I'd say. Could have been shrapnel, you wouldn't be here now if it was.'

I must say I didn't fully agree with the sergeant on that one, I didn't feel particularly lucky.

'I'm guessing you're with the 88th RFA?' continued the sergeant. 'They were fighting with us out there yesterday.'

'In all honesty sergeant, I'm not sure. I must have banged my head when I got shot as I can't remember a bloody thing.' I thought it best to continue with that line for a while.

'Well, Fritz has certainly caught us on the hop this time,' explained the sergeant. 'Their big push came two days ago and we've been fighting backwards ever since. I've 'eard that Gough's lot caught it bad just south of St Quentin and they've been routed. Doesn't bode too well for us at all. Back in the New Year I thought bloody 1918 was going to see us finish this bloody war. Don't look like it now does it? Our orders are to move back through Bapaume today and dig in again just west of the village. Don't expect you'll be doing much fighting for a while though, lucky bastard. Ah, 'ere comes the medics with the stretcher. They've been a bit rushed off their feet lately, poor sods.'

Well, at least now I know we're supposed to be in 1918, I guess that's something and there he goes with all that lucky stuff again. I suppose luck is all relative, I thought.

The sergeant leaned over and stubbed his cigarette out casually in the bottom of a brass shell casing that had been strategically placed in a white hand which was sticking out of the side wall of the trench. I hadn't noticed it there before. It was a very white hand with the palm turned upwards. Some poor beggar has been buried in the mud there and the earth had broken away revealing his hand. It was a delicate sensitive hand with long straight fingers, now bleached white from exposure to the weather, possibly a musician's hand I thought. Again I tried not to think of the wife or mother back at home just longing to hold this hand again. It seemed callous to put the make-do ashtray in the hand like that, but I guess being surrounded by death every day the guys here have just become hardened to it all. Black humour indeed. It made my stomach turn.

The stretcher bearers laid the stretcher on the ground next to me and with one at each end, they unceremoniously lifted me and part dragged me onto the stretcher. I cried out in pain. One of the stretcher bearers then knelt down to inspect my leg a little more closely.

'I think we might as well leave this strapped up as it is and just get him straight to the ADS as quick as we can. No doubt Fritz will be coming at us again soon?' He said to his colleague.

'What's an ADS?' I asked the stretcher bearer who had just spoken.

'Your first port of call mate, the local Advanced Dressing Station, the ADS. It's back near Bapaume village, but don't worry, it ain't far. At least it ain't now. It would have been a fair old way back from the old front line but since Fritz's big push two days back, when our front lines were overrun, we've been moving backwards. It's complete chaos mate. You're sitting in our old rear trenches at the moment,' the stretcher bearer explained.

With that, the stretcher bearers casually lifted me up from the floor of the trench, and we left, in the same direction that Karl had been taken.

The stretcher bearer was right, the journey to the ADS was chaotic. The stretcher bearers tried to make their way along the winding zig zagging trenches as best as they could, but shells were starting to come in thick and fast now and men were running about shouting, obviously preparing themselves for yet another attack by the Germans. We definitely seemed to be going against the general flow of traffic. With soldiers continuously running towards us we were bumped and knocked about and twice one of the stretcher bearers dropped me, groaning into the mud. I have no idea how they knew where they were going in the chaos, but they seemed to.

With all the activity and noise going on, and the constant stress from the risk of a shell landing on top of you, it was hard to think at all. I was just going with it, everything seemed to be out of my control anyhow. I also felt very sleepy, in a drugged, confused sort of way. I knew my leg was badly smashed up but I didn't even know if I was actually hurt anywhere else. I didn't think so, but with all the pain from my leg I'm not sure I would have known anyway. Either way, I probably had lost a lot of blood and maybe even had the beginnings of an infection. I certainly didn't feel so good, which certainly wasn't a good sign. I think I had been running on adrenaline up until now and the full pain and fear of my new reality was starting to hit me.

Suddenly, as we rounded a corner in the trench there was an even louder shriek and a crash. The trench in front of us took a direct hit. The two stretcher bearers went down taking me with them onto the floor of the trench. The earth reeled and rocked about us, it felt as if we were trapped in a sea of boiling mud and bodies. Above the ear splitting crash of the shell I could hear an unearthly scream of pain and fear from someone close by. It soon stopped so I guessed whoever it was, it was probably his last communication with this world.

'Shovels! Shovels! Quick, men buried!' Came the cries from all around me.

'Stretcher bearers! Stretcher bearers! Here quick!' More shouts. Shells were still whistling and banging all around us. The noise was indescribable. A constant whizz-whizz-whizz, bang-bang-bang. The ground was rolling now and I just lay there in the bottom of what was left of the trench with my hands held tightly over my head - there was no more I could do, it was all down to luck now. Eventually the crashing and banging moved on up the trench and away from us. Some other poor bastards were getting it now I thought. I tried to sit up and move my arms and leg. I didn't think I had been wounded again, I had been lucky. A not so lucky soldier crawled painfully along the floor of the trench beside me, on his stomach, dragging his shattered legs behind him. He had no trousers on anymore, just his blood soaked underpants. One of my stretcher bearers got up and crawled over to him to see what he could do.

'No,' the man moaned. 'I'm all right mate, go and see to old Charlie, he was right behind me, I think he's hurt bad, I'm alright.'

I just looked at the soldiers shattered legs. There was nothing left below his knees. I looked at what was left of the trench behind him and there was no one there, just shreds of what might have once been a uniform. If old Charlie had been there he had obviously been vaporised. I just felt cold. Maybe it was the soldier's way, of always looking out for their mates and putting them first, or maybe it was just denial, an instinct to shut out the horror of his own injuries? Either way the poor bastard didn't look like he had long left in this sorry world. My two stretcher bearers did their best to tourniquet his legs in an attempt at stopping the flow of blood. There was little else they could do for him really. He needed urgent hospital treatment and he wouldn't be getting that here. Another young soldier sitting against the muddy trench wall looked ghastly. His mouth and nose had been sliced by shrapnel. His top lip had been completely cut away from his teeth and blood was pouring from his face and filling his gas respirator which he still had partially on. He was choking and shuddering. My stretcher bearer lifted his head up gently and then blood started to pour and gurgle out of his mouth in great bubbles. His eyes were full of fear and pain. The stretcher bearer managed to remove the gas respirator and secured a big padded dressing against the man's face to try and staunch the flow of blood.

'Don't worry mate, we'll be back for you, you'll be just fine,' promised the stretcher bearer, smiling.

Amid the confusion and the continuous cries for help, shovels and stretcher bearers, my two bearers quickly lifted me up back onto my stretcher and we were away again, over the mangled, muddy remains of the trench and the soldiers.

We eventually came out of the underground surreal world of the trenches into what passed for a wide open space. In reality, although the claustrophobic trench walls had gone - which was certainly a relief - all there now seemed to be as far as the eye could see were vast stretches of mud everywhere. Flat mud, piled up mud, mud tracks, mud roads and mud walking about disguised as human beings and horses. There was absolutely no colour, no greenery at all. The noise was still deafening though. There was the constant roar of the guns and the shrieking of the shells flying overhead, the inevitable explosions going off all around, the cries, and the awful sound of horses and mules shrieking. There was also the constant shouting and shrilling of whistles and men running here, there and everywhere, but most disturbing for me was the smell. The all-pervading smell of gas and sulphur, mixed with the stench of rotting corpses clung to everything. Even with my eyes closed I could smell and taste it with every breath. I wanted to gag constantly; I shall never forget that awful smell.

There were planes flying overhead and the ack-ack guns were following their progress, spitting out pretty puffs of black smoke which appeared in the sky all around them. I saw a dogfight high up in the sky somewhere over what I thought would be the enemy lines. A small plane climbed up and then swooped down to the enemy below, I couldn't make out which side was which. Away in the distance I saw a plane come tumbling down, like a falling dead bird. Poor bastard, whoever he was.

The stretcher bearers placed me down outside a large dark green tent, at the end of a line of other men lying on stretchers. Before I even had a chance to thank them, they had run off to collect another stretcher lying in a big pile of empty ones next to the tent and were disappearing back into the entrance to the trenches again at full pelt. I hoped they would be able to pick up that wounded soldier and save him. I had nothing but utter awe for those men, constantly in danger while saving the lives of others. I felt truly humbled.

I looked down the long line of men lying next to me. Some were sitting up smoking, others were laying down and moaning in pain, and many were just laying still, possibly dead. The worst were the gassed soldiers who had been set to one side. They seemed to be constantly writhing in agony with their mouths and throats burning from the inside, hacking up blood and foam from destroyed lungs and often tearing the skin from their necks in a desperate attempt to pull the gas from their lungs. They were begging and pleading just to die. There was no hope for them. One man, lying in a small group of gassed soldiers at the end of the row was screaming and screaming and clawing at himself until no more sound came out, then he simply - thankfully - died. Two orderlies came over and lifted him away to one side and then they covered his head and mouth with mud, presumably to prevent the gasses in his lungs from contaminating anyone else? Maybe it would have been better if someone had put the mud over his head and mouth and ended his misery for him hours ago? That would have been more humane. Many more men simply sat there quietly with their eyes open, staring into space. Perhaps shock had set in with them, I felt like it had with me. I had often read and heard about the 'thousand yard stare' that many men seem to have when coming out of battle, it has often been captured in photographs. I think I finally understood what was behind that stare. They had seen too much.

I looked up at the blueness of the sky again and noticed that the dogfight had now edged closer. Even above the noise on the ground I could hear the chatter of the machine guns from the planes. One of the planes, a German I think, but it may have been one of ours, started to belch out thick black smoke and then a fiery ball dropped away from the plane.

'Petrol tank that is, he's just dropped his burning petrol tank,' commented the soldier lying next to me, who was also watching the dogfight with interest.

The plane tried to flatten out and glide down but his wings were burning fiercely now and the machine was rocking violently from side to side as the pilot desperately tried to get his burning craft under control. We could see the gunner in the rear frantically throwing things over the side, probably ammunition I thought. He disappeared over the horizon and we saw a huge flash, probably as he hit the ground. There was a thick column of black smoke reaching up into the sky, the last evidence of his dramatic fiery fall. Just another two poor bastards going to a horrible end I thought.

At that moment a nurse came out of the tent and walked along the line of men. She oozed efficiency and had a clipboard in her hand which she was looking at and asking questions of one or two of the men as she moved along. I'm not sure what I really expected a war nurse would look like. I think I might have had a romantic image of a sylph like beautiful figure, drifting amongst the men, tending to their needs. This was certainly nothing like that. She had on a heavy brown coat, thick woollen gloves, a knitted balaclava with a sort of blue knitted cap on top of her head and she had heavy hobnailed shoes on her feet with a pair of heavy woollen socks pulled over them. A romantic image it most certainly wasn't. However, despite that, I could still recognise that she was a woman, and one with a beautiful smile at that. After all the explosions, the bullets, the gas, the mud, the blood and the mutilated men, she was certainly a sight for sore eyes.

Finally she came and stood in front of me.

'Ah a new boy. How are you feeling?'

'Not too bad nurse, I've had better days but not too bad.'

It's funny isn't it? Back in my life in 1984 my wounds would have been worthy of a team of highly trained paramedics rushing me across town, blue lights flashing, delivering me to the nearest hospital where I would have been greeted by the finest surgeons and nurses, just waiting to whisk me straight into theatre to rebuild me again. Here, even I had started to feel ashamed at my comparatively puny wound. Looking at the wrecks of men around me, I almost felt like a fraud.

The nurse looked me up and down quickly with what seemed like a much practised eye.

'Let's have a look at that leg soldier,' she said as she was bending down to kneel beside me.

'Mmmm, from what I can see it looks like quite a large wound to the right knee, tissue damage and some obvious bone damage I think. Not pretty my lad, but we'll soon have you patched up.'

She stood up again and pulled a pencil from the top of the clipboard.

'What's your name and number corporal?' She asked.

'Em George Puttnam,' I stumbled, still trying to digest what she had just said.

'I can't remember my number but I know I'm with the RFA,' I stated, almost proudly.

The nurse eyed me strangely. She stepped forward and knelt down again to look around my head.

'Have you had any concussion Corporal?' She asked as she pulled the cord from around my neck to look at the number on my dog tags.

'Ah yes nurse, I think I must have banged my head a bit, I've been a little confused,' I lied.

'Hmm yes, you probably just need some rest and you'll soon be back in the pink. We can't do much for you here as everything's in chaos. This used to be a main dressing station but we started pulling out two days ago when Jerry started their big attack. Most of our medical team are now back at the main station in Albert. We'll get you over there as soon as we can and the doctors will have a proper look at you. You may need an op on that knee. I'll have one of my nurses bring you something to help with the pain and they will dress up and splint your leg, then we'll get you moved on. One of the field ambulances should be along in the next twenty minutes or so and we'll get you on that, hopefully before Fritz gets here.'

With that she smiled broadly at me, turned, walked quickly away and disappeared back into the tent.

As I lay there I managed to look down at myself. I could definitely smell the stench of urine, dampness and decay coming from my body. I think I must have pissed myself at some point judging from the smell, probably when I was shot I thought, not that I would remember that. I could also definitely see things moving around in my uniform. They looked like very small maggots, or lice or something. Once I started to look closely it became obvious there were hundreds of the things, possibly thousands. Uuuugh! Disgusting! I thought, I just had to get out of this nauseating uniform. I started to scratch.

At that point, another similarly dressed nurse carrying a large canvas bag over her shoulder and a big bowl in her arms came out of the tent and walked over to me.

'Hello George, my name's Helen. I've come to do your dressing,' she smiled as she kneeled down next to me.

Nurse Helen, who couldn't have been more than 19 years of age, swiftly cut away the puttee that was bound around my leg and the rifle. Discarding these and placing the rifle carefully to one side she then cut away my trousers to just above my knee. She washed around the wound using the hot water from the bowl and some clean white linen cloth, which didn't stay clean for very long. It was a grim job and the smell from my body was becoming almost overpowering, even for me. The nurse took a small canteen bottle out of her bag and gave it to me.

'Drink a few big gulps of this, it'll help with the pain,' she smiled.

I did as I was told and immediately my eyes started to fill up and I was coughing again.

'What is this stuff?' I asked.

'Ah sorry, it's brandy, but it's pretty rough I'll admit. It should help you relax a bit though. Do you have any cigarettes on you?'

I was just about to respond again, almost apologetically, saying I didn't smoke, but before I could even open my mouth nurse Helen reached over and patted both of my tunic breast pockets. Finding what she was looking for she opened one pocket and took out a small packet of what looked like cigarettes, and a small box of matches. It said Woodbines on the packet. She placed a cigarette in my mouth and lit it while I tried to drag in the smoke, desperately trying to avoid all the embarrassing coughing this time.

'There, that will help calm you as well. Now comes the nasty part, this is going to sting a bit,' she said as she pulled a big bottle of iodine from the bag.

Sting? Now that was an understatement if ever there was one. I nearly passed out when she started cleaning the wound with the iodine. I took a few more big drags on my cigarette, and I didn't cough quite so much this time. Nurse Helen finished up by placing a dressing over the wound and binding that up with a huge long white bandage, deftly pinning it with two safety pins. She picked all her bits up and stuffed them back into her bag, threw that over her shoulder, picked up her bowl, smiled at me and then she was gone.

Amidst all of the noise and the chaos I laid back down on the stretcher and tried to make myself comfortable.

I could hear the whiz-bang of shells creeping closer again.

'Hear that mate?' said the soldier next to me again.

'What's that?' I asked.

'Hear that dud? That's six duds in that last batch of shells,' he said.

'That's good isn't it?' I asked, naively.

'Where have you been corporal?' He responded. 'No it's not so good, gas shells sound like duds, and they make a sort of phutt sound when they land. They have just enough explosive in them to burst the case and release the gas without scattering it. Six duds like that might just mean a gas attack, we've had a few in this part of the trench already this morning,' he warned as he pulled his gas mask out of its case in readiness. I nervously did the same, not that I had any idea as to how to put the damn thing on though.

A short while later there was a lot more activity around me. Three large ambulance trucks with big red crosses on the sides pulled into the area in front of the big green tent, belching thick smoke from the exhaust pipes. The trucks looked very old fashioned to me but I guessed here in 1918 they were probably state of the art vehicles. Medical orderlies started running around loading stretchers into the back of the first truck, supervised by the first nurse I had seen. The stretchers were being loaded into a rack inside the back of the vehicle, two wide, two high and from what I could see, about four deep. A nurse jumped down from the back of the ambulance, the doors were slammed shut and the vehicle pulled away again, bouncing down the muddy track road. The same process took place with the second ambulance and very soon that too was bouncing off into the distance. Then they started loading the last ambulance. Just as I thought it was starting to look pretty full, two orderlies came over to me, picked me up and laid me down again next to another stretcher on the mud at the rear of the last ambulance. I guessed we were the last two casualties who were going to get loaded on this run. The guy next to me looked to be in a bad way. His head was almost totally covered with bandages, with holes cut out for his mouth and nose. His hands and arms were also bandaged heavily. All of his bandages were stained with fresh red blood. Just as they lifted him to load him into the rear of the ambulance there was an ear splitting shriek and a huge roar. I felt more than saw the explosion. The wave of concussion blew me about six feet away from the ambulance. Everything then fell strangely silent. At least, I thought it was. Everyone was again running around in chaos and I could see the lips of one of the stretcher bearers moving fast, so I presumed he was shouting, but all I could hear was ringing in my own ears. The stretcher bearer was now kneeling over his colleague who appeared to be covered in blood. I'm not sure if it was his own or not. The bandaged man on the stretcher was laying at an odd angle on the floor and most of his left side now appeared to be missing. His arm was gone too. There was fresh blood all over him and on the mud beneath. The two stretcher bearers ran back to collect me and soon had me loaded onto the ambulance, right next to the rear doors. It seemed like the one covered in blood was OK, it apparently wasn't his blood. He was lucky, for now. Another one of the stretcher bearers started to close the rear doors.

'Wait a mo,' shouted another voice. 'One more to go in.'

We seemed to wait for ages. I laid there looking out of the back of the ambulance when suddenly I spotted Karl, the German. He was sitting on the side of a cart about thirty feet away from me smoking a cigarette. His head was partially bandaged now. That was good, at least they were taking care of him. I instinctively waved and tried to attract his attention but I noticed he was deep in conversation with what looked to be his guard. My eyes were attracted to the guard for a moment and a feeling of fear washed over me suddenly when I recognised him. He would have just been another soldier if it hadn't been for his easily recognisable features. That crooked nose and those dark eyes. He was Violet's sinister looking soldier from 1984. He had his helmet in his hands and I noticed he had a thick shock of unruly jet black hair. It was long, too long for a soldier. He was tall, very tall but quite skinny and looked lanky and awkward with his movements. I laid there stunned. Just then two stretcher bearers came running up with another stretcher and slid it into the rack next to me. I looked across and immediately felt sick to the pit of my stomach with what I saw. It wasn't the soldier with the bandages now, or even a soldier at all, it was the nurse, Helen. Her head had been partially bound and she was covered in blood. Her coat, uniform and hat had all gone, probably blown away in the force of the explosion. She lay there in just a bra and what was left of some kind of linen under-skirt. All soaked in her blood. A brown great coat was placed over her by the stretcher bearer before he closed the doors. She looked to be unconscious. I was truly horrified. She then moaned and rolled her head around. All thought of the sinister soldier forgotten for the moment, I reached across and took Helen's hand gently in mine. The engine revved up hard and the ambulance pulled away, bouncing down the muddy track. Through the windows I could see that the road we were on was only distinguishable from the surrounding shell-ploughed mud by an unbroken edging of smashed motors, ambulances, guns, carts and dead horses and mules.

I hoped we were going somewhere a little safer.

We must have been bouncing along for an hour or two, with the ambulance continually slipping and sliding in the rutted muddy road. I slept fitfully off and on, and held Nurse Helen's hand virtually the whole way. I think she woke at least once and I saw her uncovered tearful right eye looking at me. I think I even caught a slight smile on her blood covered lips. I squeezed her hand a little harder but I wanted to hug her. She coughed and blood bubbled out of her pretty mouth.

Eventually, after what seemed like several gruelling hours the ambulance slowed and stopped. The rear doors were pulled open and light flooded into the back of the ambulance. A number of medical orderlies were standing at the open doors and they started to pull the stretchers out. Obviously Nurse Helen and I were the first out. I blinked in the strong sunlight. It was a fine day with clear blue skies, sunny, but with a real chill in the air - they are the type of days I love the best. Looking around me I could see we were in the middle of a huge square with lines of large khaki green tents all around us. There were many medical orderlies and nurses hurrying around, but it seemed somewhat more organised than the casualty station at the front. I could hear the whine and crash of explosions, but they were in the distance now. The constant threat of violent death didn't seem to be hanging over everything here. The medics were removing the stretchers in a less hurried and more sympathetic way. Another nurse, huddled up in her big brown great coat, was looking at a clipboard and was calling out instructions to the teams of medics carrying the stretchers off the ambulances. I was hurried away and lost sight of Nurse Helen.

I laid back on the stretcher and looked at an aeroplane flying very slowly overhead, again followed by the crump crump and puffs of black smoke of the anti-aircraft fire. I still had no idea which side the aeroplanes were on and who was trying to shoot them down.

'Loads of archie up today eh mate? That's Fritz up there, planning their next bloody attack I shouldn't wonder,' said the medic carrying my stretcher.

'Archie?' I wondered.

'Yep, that's our lot, firing archie up at them. Not much hope of bloody hitting 'em though. Most of it just rains back down on us again!'

With a last look at the clear blue sky I was carried into the gloom of one of the nearer tents. Inside there were four rows of small low military camp beds running the length of the tent. There seemed to be patients in each one of the beds. Most were lying flat but a few were sitting up with curls of smoke hanging over their heads as they puffed furiously at their various cigarettes, cigars and pipes. A few nurses were wandering around, tending to the patients. As I was carried along one of the rows I looked at the soldiers laying there. To my untrained eye most of the injuries were pretty horrendous, missing arms, missing legs, smashed heads and bloody chests, but there seemed to be very few of those frightening gas cases. That was a blessing as it was horrendous to witness and did nothing for morale, and they were the ones that upset me the most. In the tent there was no complaining, no screaming. Just low moans coming from some of the soldiers and a few delirious rants here and there. There was a strange, almost serene atmosphere in that tent.

I was placed carefully on a bunk at the end of the row. The orderly who had been chatting to me pulled out his packet of cigarettes, lit two of them and placed one in my lips.

'Ere mate, take this, it'll help you. Take care, we'll see you around, you'll soon be in the pink,' and then he was off.

I really needed to get used to this smoking lark.

I lay there in the quiet, reasonably comfortable; blowing smoke up at the ceiling, feeling not a little light headed and trying to ignore the sounds of what could only be rats scurrying about beneath my bunk. For the first time since I'd arrived in this nightmare it was quiet, peaceful almost, and I was able to try and gather my thoughts. I thought about the nightmare of the past day. Maybe that is what it was, just a nightmare? Would I wake up some time soon back in my flat in Berkhampsted? Had I perhaps been drugged by that soldier? But how had he broken in? Was I still George Gade? Was I now someone else? Was my previous life just a dream and this was reality? My head started to spin, so I stopped thinking and decided to do something practical, like go through my pockets and see what other surprises were hidden in there, like my Woodbine cigarettes and box of Lucifer matches.

I started by looking through the large lower pockets of my tunic, which I handled with some trepidation. The lice were crawling freely all over the tunic now and it turned my stomach. I found a fairly plain but very sharp knife with a wooden handle. I found an old tin which had a picture of some old Queen I'd never seen before on it and the words 'Christmas 1914' on the front. The tin was half full of a strong smelling tobacco and a pack of cigarette papers. I also found a couple of dirty linen rags, and a few coins, large pennies with King George V's face on them.

The top breast pockets were more revealing. I found what appeared to be my army pay book, 'for use on active service' it stated clearly on the front. I opened up the dark brown book and found a whole load of new information about me, or whoever I now was. It stated that my name is George William Puttnam, regimental number 99243, a shoeing corporal in the Royal Field Artillery, 88th battalion. It says that my date of attestation - which

I can only guess was my date of joining up - was 29th March 1915 and my daily rate of pay totalled one shilling and eleven pence, which included my additional one penny per day for war pay. The next few pages had records of my weekly pay, which seemed to average out at between 10 and 15 Francs per week. Wow! All this fun and we get paid too. The last page contained my will. It appears that I have left everything to my wife in the event of my death, a Mrs Violet Daisy Puttnam of 9 George Street, Berkhampsted. My wife?? I turned the last page and there tucked in the back cover was a small white lace handkerchief inside of which was a small sepia photograph of a beautiful auburn haired young woman holding a little baby girl in her arms. Obviously a posed studio photograph. I instinctively turned the photo over and there was a penciled inscription on the back. It said *'To my darling George, please keep safe and come home to me again. We love you. Violet xxx'*

'Whew,' I said aloud. That's a heart wrencher!'

'What is?' asked the nurse who had just walked up to my bunk.

I showed her the photo and she read the inscription on the back.

'She is beautiful isn't she? Is she your wife?'

I paused for a moment before confirming that she was indeed my wife. Never even having had a steady girlfriend before it sounded strange coming from my lips.

'Well then, you had certainly better get back to her safely hadn't you?' she said as she passed the photo back to me.

I thought about that for a while.

'Yes, I suppose I had better,' I said. My mind was whirling around again now. Violet? George? Pieces of the hazy jigsaw were starting to fit together. Am I now supposed to be George, the husband of old Violet, the one who never came back from the front? What was happening here? I wish I knew.

'I need to start filling out some forms now Corporal, and being as you've got your pay book out can you pass it over so I can copy some of the details?'

I handed over the pay book, but held onto the photo.

'Here, while I'm doing the paperwork, take this Dorothy bag and put all your personal stuff in it. You can also drink this, it'll do you good,' she said, handing me a large canvas bag with a drawstring top and a large white tin mug.

As soon as I raised the mug to my mouth I could smell the strong alcohol again.

'Brandy?' I asked.

'Yes, it'll keep the pain down.'

'Not that I mind the brandy but don't you have any morphine or anything like that? And I don't want to tell you how to do your job or anything but shouldn't I be taking some antibiotics or something in case of infection?' I said, trying not to sound too ungrateful.

The nurse laughed. 'Sorry no, morphine is only for the very serious cases, yours is just a scratch,' she smiled. 'And what's antibiotics?' She asked, looking confused.

'Oh never mind, what's your name nurse?' I mumbled, trying to change the subject and trying even harder to remember when antibiotics and all that penicillin stuff had actually been invented. I thought it must have been by now, in 1918, but I wasn't sure.

'Lucy, and you're George, nice to meet you George,' she said, smiling again. 'Now come on, drink up that Brandy, I want to have a look at that wound and it might hurt a bit.'

I did as I was told and laid back down again. My head was going around in circles and I felt very tired.

Lucy finished writing up her forms and then changed my dressing, without too much discomfort on my part. She said that apart from the splintered bone fragments she could see, the wound itself looked quite clean and the bleeding seemed to have almost stopped. She took my empty cup and I put the photo and my pay book back in my new Dorothy bag. Strange name that for a bag I thought, I must look it up sometime and see why it's called that.

'Nurse, before you go, what happened to the young nurse who came in with me on the ambulance? Her name was Helen.'

'Ah, she didn't make it I'm afraid George, poor girl, damn shame.'

I laid there for a while with tears running down my cheeks, just listening to the troubling noises around me; the quiet painful moaning, the hacking and coughing of those poor bastards who had been gassed, the occasional loud ramblings of a shell-shocked or fever filled soldier, and of course the rats, until I finally drifted off into an exhausted sleep.

I was eventually woken when Nurse Lucy returned with a doctor. At least that's who I thought he must be. He was dressed in what looked like an officer's uniform, long brown leather boots and a white doctor's coat over the top, which had numerous blood stains all over it. He started to speak but my eyes were transfixed on the absolutely huge bushy handlebar moustache which was stuck to his top lip and curling up either side of his nose.

'Good morning Corporal, I'm Captain Poulton. I'm your doctor.' He said, holding out his hand to shake mine.

I reached out and we shook hands firmly.

'I'm just going to take a look at that leg of yours,' he said as he started to remove the bandage.

I fumbled around in my tunic pocket - which was now hanging next to my bunk - and took out my packet of Woodbine's and matches. I put a cigarette in my mouth and lit it, trying to be as casual as I could. I was determined not to start the habit but there wasn't much else in the way of pain relief around here and I felt that it helped a bit, even if it was just psychological.

'OK Corporal,' boomed the doctor as he straightened back up. 'Gunshot wound, straight through your knee, old man. It's a reasonably clean wound but it has shattered your knee cap and shards of bone are everywhere. I think we should be able to save the leg but you're going to need an operation to remove the bone fragments and to pin the knee joint together. You'll most likely not be able to bend your knee again but hopefully you'll be up and walking again in a few months. It's better than losing it eh? We won't be able to do it here though, we'll move you on to our general hospital in Rouen for that, and then it's back to Blighty for you old boy,' he said, with what I think passed for a smile under that gigantic moustache.

'Nurse, can you replace the dressing again and include a splint please, and then get it organised to move him onto Rouen?'

And with that, he walked briskly away. Nurse Lucy set about replacing my dressing and bandages.

'OK George, that's all done, you lay here and try to relax. I'll get everything sorted and I'll be along again shortly with another brandy for you. At least we have plenty of that here, and I think we'll probably have you on your way to Rouen in the morning. There are ambulance trains running all the time from here'.

She smiled and walked away, leaving me alone again to contemplate everything that had happened to me in the past 24 hours; this nightmare, my wound, the thought of possibly losing my leg or at the very least not being able to bend it ever again. I needed another cigarette, and then I noticed I only had two left. My luck was definitely out; I had just started smoking and nearly run out already.

I think I slept then for many hours. I was totally exhausted and the brandy and cigarettes were having an effect too. Not sure if it was all good but it seemed to knock me out, which I think was probably what I needed. The next thing I remember was being woken up by a young medical orderly with a tray of food for me. I'd forgotten that the last meal I'd had was that pie and chips back in my flat in1984 and I was starving. I tucked into the cold boiled spuds, the slab of bacon covered in cold fat and the sloppy scrambled eggs and toast as if it was a Michelin star meal. It certainly tasted like it.

After breakfast I busied myself by going through my pockets and putting anything I could find safely inside my new Dorothy bag. It seemed like all the other soldiers around me had done the same and it appeared that everyone was very protective of their Dorothy bags. Not too long after that two stretcher bearers arrived at my bunk.

'Good morning Corporal, we're off now, get your things,' one of them said.

The only 'things' I had were my tunic jacket and my new bag, so I grabbed these and I was good to go. As we went outside I thought I'd be put back into one of those awful ambulances again, but we walked off between two of the tents and when we came out the other side I was absolutely amazed to see that we were right next to a huge black steam train sitting right behind the tents. The carriages were all painted dark green and there were bright red and white medical crosses painted all along the sides. Wow I thought, that's good planning. I had to give the military credit where it was due, the evacuation of wounded soldiers seemed to be a well-planned and structured process, thankfully. I guessed they had had lots of practice.

I was loaded onto one of the carriages and my stretcher was strapped down into a rack which was three layers high. The orderly hung my tunic and my Dorothy bag on the rack next to me and then he left. The train carriage seemed like a smaller version of the dressing tent; it certainly seemed quite well equipped and all very efficient. I had my last cigarette while the rest of the train was being loaded with the wounded and just before we pulled off an orderly came around and gave every man a large mug of rum. Well, it wasn't the best and it certainly stung my throat at 08.00 in the morning, but at least it made a bloody change from brandy. I couldn't see the NHS I knew and loved issuing mugs of rum to their patients.

Chapter Four

Rouen, France - 27 March 1918

I had slept for most of the journey but I awoke to the sound of brakes squealing and steam hissing as we pulled into what I presumed was Rouen station. I looked out of the window but couldn't see much. There were soldiers and orderlies milling around outside the window and I could hear whistles being blown and people shouting. After what seemed like a wait of hours, they finally began unloading the train. I was loaded down onto the platform and straight into the back of what looked like a horse drawn ambulance with seven other men. The doors were banged shut and off we went again. We were only in the ambulance for about ten minutes when it pulled up and the doors were opened again.

'Welcome to Rouen Racecourse,' shouted a beaming medical orderly who had on a slightly different uniform to all the others I had seen so far.

'And welcome to the 1st Australian General Hospital,' he said with what I now realised was a thick Australian accent.

I looked around and we did indeed seem to be on what was obviously once a very large racecourse. There were rows and rows of large green tents for as far as the eye could see, stretching all around what would have once been the race track. In the middle of all the tents I could see what was once the racecourse buildings and the grandstand now covered in red and white crosses and with the Australian flag flying high above for all to see. It was certainly a sight to behold.

We were quickly removed from the ambulance, and my seven new mates and I were taken into the nearest tent and laid carefully onto the nearest available hospital beds. This tent was absolutely massive compared to the one back in Albert and was full of wounded soldiers.

A nurse came up to me and introduced herself as Louise, again in a thick Aussie accent. She had with her the inevitable clip board and asked me my name, rank, serial number, blah, blah, blah. I remembered everything off by heart. Even I was starting to believe I was a corporal in the British army now. With that done, she quickly moved onto the next patient and went through the same process with him.

'All very efficient,' I thought.

Before long, Nurse Louise was back.

'Let's get you sorted now Corporal,' she said.

With that she proceeded to take off my lice infested tunic jacket and then removed my boots and socks, which were also very probably lice infested. It was a bit of a struggle to get them off but what a relief it was. The only problem was I could literally see the smell coming from my feet as if it were a thick green haze. The stench was unbearable; I would bet that Nurse Louise wished she'd been wearing her gas mask today. She then removed what was left of my trousers, cutting most of them away with her sharp scissors, and also embarrassingly enough, cutting away my grey long johns too - which had possibly started out as white? I couldn't be sure. I've never worn long johns in my life, I didn't even know I had them on.

I watched her while she worked. She was a very pretty young girl, too pretty and too young to have to deal with all these horrors, and I felt sure she had probably already seen enough horror here to last a lifetime, several lifetimes in fact. She stripped off my khaki coloured shirt and grey undershirt with well-practised moves and I was finally laying completely naked on the bed, save for my dressing and bandages of course. Nurse Louise then left and came quickly back with a large steaming bowl of hot water and some clean towels and proceeded to wash me all over, leaving no part untouched. It took at least four changes of water before my white skin even started to become visible through the layers of mud and dried blood. Despite my injuries, and perhaps inevitably, things started to get quite exciting when she began to wash me between my legs.

'Looks like someone is feeling better?' she smiled broadly, winked and gave me a flick with her flannel before quickly moving on to wash my chest. Embarrassing moment over, I swiftly changed the subject.

'So, why is this called the Australian hospital Louise, and why am I here?'

'Well, it's called the 1st Australian General Hospital Rouen because it is mostly staffed by volunteer medical staff from Australia, we all volunteered and came out here together to set up this hospital. But we don't just fix up the Aussie soldiers, we take anyone, see, we even took you,' she said smiling.

'Where are you from Louise, you're a long way from home?'

'I'm from Brisbane and yes it's my first time away. My parents weren't happy at first, but I just had to do something and I think all in all they're kind of proud of me.'

'I bet they are Louise, and I'm certainly grateful you're here,' I said, smiling at her.

When she had finished washing me, Nurse Louise produced a pair of red and white striped pyjamas and started to dress me in them. I have to say; they felt so much more comfortable than that bloody old lice infested uniform of mine. They were that flannelette type you see in all the old movies, with a thick white cord around the waist which you had to tie in a bow to hold them up. Maybe elastic hadn't been invented yet? I wondered.

'You'll be going for your operation sometime this afternoon,' she said. 'The orderlies will come and get you about half an hour before and take you over to the theatre. It'll all be over in no time at all and you'll soon be back in the pink. I'm going to take your tunic for a quick delousing, you'll have it back in a few hours but can you make sure you've taken everything out of the pockets for me? Meanwhile, is there anything else you need?'

I smiled at her with what I hoped was my best seductive look. 'Yes, some cigarettes and a nice whisky,' I said, only half joking, as I took everything from my tunic and placed it all in my new Dorothy bag and handed the tunic to Nurse Louise.

'All right I'll see what I can do, just for you mind,' she said, smiling as she walked away, holding my tunic at arm's length.

'Mmmm with my current levels of hygiene I had more chance of catching cholera than I did of catching the wonderful nurse Louise,' I mumbled to myself.

True to her word, less than five minutes later she was back with a packet of Players Navy Cut cigarettes and a mug.

'Thank you Louise, I really do appreciate that. I need to pay for those cigarettes, but I'm not sure if I have any money on me,' I said, reaching out for my Dorothy bag again.

'No worries Corporal, they're supplied for the patients. See you later.'

'Thanks again Nurse Louise, you wonderful person,' I called after her.

I swigged back the mug of rum - not whisky, but beggars can't be choosers I guess - then lit up a cigarette and laid back. I reached over and took out the picture of my family - the one that I never knew I had - from my bag. My 'wife' sure looks beautiful I thought. I wondered if this was the same Violet from the hospice. I guessed in this dream or parallel universe or whatever it was, it must be. Either way, she looked lovely and very happy. Just staring at her beautiful face cheered me up no end.

I then started to give some thought to what was going to happen when I got back to England. Where would they send me next? Would I be going home to Violet and the baby? How would all that work? Or would I find a way to get back to my home in 1984 before then? I hoped so as this was getting all too difficult, and not to mention painful.

At some point during the afternoon two orderlies came to take me over to the operating theatre. They carefully lifted me onto a stretcher with one swift and very well-practised movement, took me out of the tent and over to one of the racecourse buildings. As we approached it I could see that it was a very large green painted wooden structure with two big double doors at the side. The basic drab green wooden exterior was quite deceiving as inside the building the large room was very well lit and appeared quite modern and well kitted out. There was a row of operating tables running along each wall and there were a number of doctors, nurses and orderlies bustling around. There was certainly a lot of activity going on. I was taken by the orderlies to an empty position along the right hand wall and again they expertly slid me down onto the vacant operating table. Almost immediately, a nurse with her apron covered in blood and some other stains of unmentionable origin stepped up and started to remove my pyjama trousers whilst another nurse was placing some instruments on a nearby tray. It was all much practised and extremely methodical. I guessed it had to be, there wasn't much time for anything else? A doctor appeared and introduced himself as Captain Over, a surgeon with the 2nd Australian Division. His white overalls were covered in blood too. As I stared transfixed at the blood stains, I started to get more than a bit apprehensive.

'I'm going to be performing the operation old mate, there's nothing to worry about,' he said as he started to look at my knee once the nurse had removed the dressing.

'Doesn't look too bad, but your knee joint is pretty shattered, you'll not be moving it about much from here on in. Still, we should be able to pin it all up and save the leg, so that's a positive isn't it?'

I knew it was a rhetorical question so I didn't bother to answer. I just smiled bleakly. Butterflies were having a battle to end all battles in my stomach and I now felt like throwing up.

'All right, let's get on with it shall we? Nurse, the chloroform please.'

'Chloroform? Wait, isn't there a general anaesthetic?' I started to say, but the nurse had already covered my mouth and nose with a damp sweet smelling cloth and was holding a brown bottle of liquid in her other hand. I felt like I couldn't breathe and I started to retch and struggle but someone else was also holding me down firmly, and then the room started to spin and I don't remember a lot more.

I woke up and could hear voices close by. It was the Aussie doctor talking to someone and it was obviously about me. He seemed to be giving an account of how the operation had gone and what his prognosis for the future was. I had the mother of all headaches and struggled to drag my very heavy eyelids open. I finally managed it and it was all a bit blurred and hazy but I could just make out the Aussie surgeon standing to my right. Next to him, was an officer of the British army who was listening intently to the doctor. With my sight clearing I recognised the British officer immediately and my heart lurched. He was quite distinctive with his awkward lanky physique and his very crooked nose and dark, sinister eyes. I tried to get up and shouted out something unintelligible. The Aussie doctor turned to me and the British officer stepped away out of my sight. I heard him thank the surgeon then he walked quickly away.

'Who was that?' I croaked.

'Oh, just the duty British officer commanding this area. He was doing his rounds and getting updates on the progress of the men. I've not met him before, he seems a good type. Now, you're all done and it's good to see you awake and looking so well. I want you to get a good night's sleep and then we'll be getting you out of here early tomorrow and on a ship home. It's not that we don't want to keep you here and look after you but Fritz is attacking along the whole front in force and our guys are still being pushed back. We're expecting a whole lot of casualties to be hitting us through the night and over the next few days, so we need the beds freed up. I'll leave you in the very capable care of the nurses and the orderlies will take you back to the ward once you're ready. Good luck Blue,' and with that, he turned and walked away, whistling some tuneless tune to himself.

All in all, I felt far from well.

I was out of it for the rest of that evening and throughout the night. Hallucinations came thick and fast along with the vivid nightmares and I'd definitely lost any sense of what was real and what wasn't, even if I thought I knew what was real anymore anyway. I'm not sure whether it was the events of the past few days, the wound, the chloroform, perhaps a slight fever or the operation itself, but I was starting to feel sweaty, hot and cold and definitely delirious. In my more lucid moments I started to worry about whether I had an infection and what that might mean here in 1918.

I was vaguely aware of being taken from the hospital tent on a stretcher at some point and loaded back onto a train again. I think I remember a long train journey, or that might have just been a dream, but I definitely do recall being unloaded down from a train and being placed on the floor for some time. I remember that distinctly as there was a bitterly cold wind howling around me and I was freezing. I remember a nurse tucking blankets around me and lighting a cigarette with great difficulty before finally putting it to my lips. I eventually managed, with a real struggle, to drag myself out of my dreamlike state and only then started to take in my surroundings. I seemed to be lying on a dockside in what looked to be a harbour, lined up along the floor with a long line of other wounded soldiers. We were lying along a dock next to a large ship which was belching black smoke from two huge yellow funnels high above us. The ship was mostly white in colour but had a distinctive bright yellow stripe painted around the side. I also noticed it had large red and white crosses painted all around her sides too. A hospital ship. I wondered if the Red Cross signs were big enough, I hoped so.

There was a lot of frantic activity and hustle and bustle going on around and on board the ship and it was fairly evident that she was being loaded and getting ready to sail. This was obviously my ride home I thought.

I remember the proudly painted sign on the side of the ship; it was the SS Saint Patrick.

Chapter Five

SS Saint Patrick - 28 March 1918

I was shuddering uncontrollably with the cold by the time my turn came around to be picked up and loaded on board. The cold was that deep chilling cold that seems to get right into the marrow of your bones. To stop myself getting too miserable I thought about what I had already been through out there at the front and convinced myself that this wasn't really so bad, and I was nearly safe. The puffing and sweating stretcher bearers ran up and down the slippery, precarious gangplank and down into the bowels of the ship carrying their wounded patients. When my turn came we descended some very steep stairs and arrived onto a wide open deck which seemed to run the full length of the ship. There were rows and rows of bunks and racks for stretchers running the length of the ship and wounded soldiers seemed to be filling most of them already. I was laid onto a bunk next to what looked to be an empty gift shop which was now filled with medical supplies. Looking around me I suspected the ship had spent a previous life as a cross channel ferry before being requisitioned for use as a hospital ship. The orderly made sure I had my tunic and my all-important Dorothy bag with me before he left and ran off down the ship to get his next load. I looked at my tunic hanging next to me and watched the lice crawling on it for a while. It had been deloused back at the hospital, but obviously they were back, and with a vengeance by the looks of it. I wondered why I still needed the bloody thing.

Walking wounded soldiers were being led in now and they were sitting down in the rows of seats in the bow end of the ship. The whole deck was a mass of men in khaki and nurses in grey and red uniforms. I couldn't see an inch of floor anywhere. The noise level was horrendous. Shouting, hollering, whistles, and the ever present moans, groans and coughing. I suspected the rats had also managed to follow us from the trenches too.

I turned and glanced at the man lying on the bunk to my right. He didn't seem like he was able to sit up and he was lying on his left side, facing me. He smiled a lopsided toothy grin at me and gingerly held out his big right hand.

'How's it going big-un, I'm John Burns, but everyone calls me Jock. What's up with you then?' the soldier asked as he indicated the bandage on my leg. He had to shout loudly to be heard above the noise of the ship and I still struggled to hear what he was saying. I wasn't surprised he was called Jock, with his mad mop of curly red hair and thick Glaswegian accent he couldn't really be anything else.

'Hi,' I said. 'I'm George, George Puttnam, pleased to meet you.'

'Where did you cop it then?' He asked.

'I'm not really sure, I think it was over near Bapaume somewhere,' I responded.

'No, I meant you, your leg is it? Shell was it?'

'Oh I see, sorry,' I grinned. 'Yep seems to be my right knee. Gunshot wound by all accounts. I've had my operation back in Rouen so hopefully I'll be on the mend again soon. You?'

'Ahhhgh, I was with the 2nd Manchesters over at St. Quentin. Copped a shell, landed right behind me, tore off most of my bloody arse. Bloody painful it is! Have you got any ciggies?'

'Yes of course mate, no problem,' I said as I reached into my pocket and took out my packet of Players. I lit two cigarettes and passed one over to Jock. I was finally getting the hang of this.

'Ta big-un,' he beamed as he took a big drag of the cigarette. 'At least we're on our way home aye?'

'Yep,' I agreed. 'Where's home for you?' I asked.

'Ah we're out on the Garscube Road, Glasgow. You?'

'I'm living in Berkhampsted, it's a small town in Hertfordshire, just off the A41, you know near the bottom of the M1 motorway,' I explained.

'Motorway? What's that?' Jock asked, somewhat confused.

I could really kick myself sometimes.

'Sorry, just a road.'

'Married?' Jock asked again. He definitely wanted to chat and I didn't mind, it took my mind off things and anyway I was already warming to Jock. I had to think about his question for a second or two. It seemed I was married here, in this time.

'Er yes, I am,' I responded.

'Kids?'

'Er yes, one, a little girl.' It actually felt very nice saying that. It gave me a strange warm feeling inside, not one that I had ever experienced before - well, apart from that time I managed to fall asleep and piss myself at Johnny's stag do, but that's a whole other story.

'Are you married Jock?' I asked.

'Nah laddie, not got around to it yet, I haven't had much opportunity over the past four years,' he laughed.

At that point there were three ear bruising blasts from the ship's horn and the engine noise increased significantly as we slipped away from the dock. The smell of diesel fumes wafted across the deck. From where Jock and I were lying on our low bunks we couldn't see a thing out of any of the portholes, just the clear blue sky and the occasional seagull floating by, but we knew we were off. We had finally left France. A loud cheer went up all along the deck and many of the men were whistling and cheering, and a few renditions broke out which were definitely not suitable for sensitive ears. They all knew that the danger wasn't over yet, but they had at least left France and were now heading home for England, one step closer to home and their loved ones.

'Where are we now and any idea where we're going?' I asked Jock.

'Aye laddie, we're at the port of Le Havre and we're sailing across to Southampton. Back to good ol' Blighty,' he grinned. 'We're bloody done with that war at last, aye laddie?'

The ship rocked as we left the harbour and ventured out into the open sea.

'I bloody hope the old Fritz subs ain't out there waiting for us with their bloody torpedoes,' Jock shouted.

'You're a barrel of bloody fun Jock,' I kidded, but I knew it was a very real threat.

The ship horn blasted again just as another rousing version of *It's a Long Way to Tipperary* began to catch on all along the deck.

Chapter Six

Malbork Castle, Prussia - 27 March 1918

Hauptmann Claus Von Schultz sat rigid with his large muscular frame crammed into the delicately upholstered Louis XIV chair. He studied the large and imposing, but extremely uninviting reception room he found himself sitting in. His unnaturally deep blue eyes were drawn to the stunning gilt and bronze chandelier hanging from the high ceiling in the centre of the room. He recognised it at once as a Baccarat. He looked around the walls which were covered in paintings by Cezanne, Kandinsky, Monet, Uccello, Malevich and Masaccio. All originals he thought, obviously. He looked out of the magnificently designed baroque style windows spanning one wall, probably by Zimmermann he guessed. The view outside was of the large cobble-stoned courtyard, from where he had just entered the castle. He had been waiting for five minutes. Hauptmann Claus Von Schultz wasn't accustomed to waiting and he felt very uncomfortable.

The large wooden door opened and in stepped the perfectly attired servant who had greeted him previously.

'The master will see you now sir.'

Von Schultz stood up to his full six foot six inches height, straightened his uniform, placed his highly polished pickelhaube helmet carefully under his left arm and followed the servant out of the room.

They marched down a long plush red carpeted corridor which was decorated with various antique pistols, muskets, cutlasses, rapiers and shields, interspersed with fine oil portraits of what appeared to be a long family line of Prussian officers. At the end of the passage way the servant finally came to a large ornately carved oak door and knocked lightly.

'The master will see you in the library sir,' he said as he opened the door and stepped inside.

'Hauptmann Von Schultz to see you master,' the servant said reverently, with his eyes fixed on the floor in front of his feet. The servant held the door open to allow Von Schultz inside and then he smartly stepped out again, closing the door quietly behind him.

Von Schultz looked briefly around the large grandiose room which was lined with floor-to-ceiling oak bookcases and had large ornate French windows which opened out onto the perfectly manicured gardens. There were two large oxblood leather armchairs placed either side of the huge stone fireplace. One of the chairs was occupied.

'Come in Herr Hauptmann, sit down here next to me,' came the voice from the chair.

Von Schultz walked across the deep pile red carpet and sat down in the indicated chair. He wasn't generally accustomed to feeling nervous, but he felt extremely ill at ease at this moment.

'Tea Herr Hauptmann?'

'No thank you sir,' said Von Schultz, studying the man in the chair opposite him, he just wanted to get this over and done with as quickly as possible. Although he had met him on one or two occasions previously, Von Schultz was still taken aback by the man's physical appearance. He was obviously very tall, but not well built. He had the appearance of being rather awkward and ungainly and had a painful looking twist to his spine when he stood. His hands and fingers were exceptionally long with pure white skin. This was definitely a man who had never seen hard labour. The most striking feature however was the man's face; it was the most emotionless face Von Schultz had ever seen. With his long, lank jet black hair, his pure white, almost translucent skin, his aquiline nose and dark, dark staring eyes, his appearance was very unnerving, even to Von Schultz.

'I hope your trip back from the front was uneventful?' asked the man.

'It was indeed uneventful, thank you sir.' In the two years since Von Schultz had first met the man he had never addressed him as anything other than sir. Von Schultz knew the man was known as Count Hermann Von Rautennburg, but despite a lot of research he had never found any real history on the count or his family lineage, despite the impressive array of portraits lining the walls of the castle. He suspected that this was an assumed name, but he also knew that the count was very well connected and a personal friend of the Kaiser, so Von Schultz hadn't pushed the research too far. He had his suspicions that this might have proved very dangerous indeed.

'So Herr Hauptmann, we have failed in our last endeavour.' As always, the count came straight to the point.

'Failed sir? I beg your pardon but I believe the mission was successful,' Von Schultz argued. 'I found Unteroffizier Karl Von Ohain as we discussed and I personally eliminated him during a routine patrol in no-man's-land. There were no witnesses. I was unfortunately unable to find the specific Tommy in the area you had suggested, but I dispatched Von Ohain with a shot to the head. You indicated that eliminating both of them would be preferable, but one would suffice?'

'I did Herr Hauptmann, you are correct. And my research showed that indeed you were initially successful, you managed to eliminate one of our targets, but not Karl Von Ohain as you believe. You did however manage to eliminate the Tommy - George Puttnam.'

Von Schultz looked puzzled and sat uneasily in his chair. 'But I never came across the Tommy, let alone eliminated him.'

'That is as maybe, but nevertheless the fact is he was eliminated and I was successful in my endeavour, for a while. However, this now seems to have been reversed. Our actions must have been noticed. This causes me a great problem.'

Von Schultz had no real idea what the count was talking about, he was totally confused.

'Herr Hauptmann, I must tell you that I am very disappointed. You will now have to go back and finish the task, but this time we must be sure and you will have to eliminate both of our targets.'

'Please accept my sincere apologies sir, but how am I to carry out your request? I left Karl Von Ohain in no-man's-land with a bullet in his head and I never found the Tommy. Where am I to find the targets now?' Von Schultz asked nervously.

'Yes it's true, your task is unfortunately even harder now Herr Hauptmann. Both of your targets are on their way back to England as we speak. You will have to follow them there and finish this.'

Von Schultz looked stunned. 'But sir, how will I get to England? We are at war, I would never make it across the channel, and even if I did I would be spotted immediately in England and shot as a spy.'

Von Schultz was being logical. His mere size, and the gnarled cutlass wound which ran from above his left eye down to his chin, coupled with the missing three fingers from his left hand, his intense blue eyes and his mop of blond hair all served to ensure he was a highly visible and memorable individual. He was certainly not one to blend easily into any background.

'You have no imagination Herr Hauptmann, you will go to England openly and above board, and in uniform. You will not be a spy; you will go as a prisoner of war.'

'But sir, if I am a prisoner of war how will I get to our targets and complete the mission? It doesn't make any sense.'

The Count started to sound a little frustrated. 'Herr Hauptmann, let me be clear, the war will finish in November of this year, which is just over seven months away. You will go from here back to the front and get yourself captured, and please try not to get yourself killed in the process, which will be of no help to me. As an officer you will definitely be questioned first and then sent straight back to England. You will remain a prisoner of war in England until you are released, as you will inevitably be, and then you will slip away and carry out your task. Both of your targets will be with you, in England. The Tommy will be residing in a small town called Berkhampsted which is in the county of Hertfordshire. I do not know where Karl Von Ohain will be incarcerated but I suspect that upon his release in England you will most likely locate him somewhere close to the Tommy. This time you will do it successfully.'

Von Schultz was reeling at this, he had so many questions, but he was also very aware of the Count's limited patience. He understood very well that the Count had some unique gifts. He knew from the last time that his target Karl Von Ohain had been exactly where the Count had said that he would be, and the events at the front had unfurled exactly as he had said they would, up until now that is. But to predict the end of the war in seven months, this was incredible.

'How can you know this sir? Are we going to be victorious, what is going to happen?' Von Schultz asked.

'I simply know these things Herr Hauptmann and no, the German army will unfortunately not be victorious on this occasion. We will eventually sign an armistice on the 11th of November this year and victory will be in the hands of the British Empire, France and the United States of America. This will be very damaging for Germany and this is the reason why your mission is so necessary. We need to change things for the future and you will be a key part of our success in the years to come. As usual, I will leave the final details of the mission to you, I don't care how you do it, just do it this time, Herr Hauptmann. As always, if you need anything, you will have it. Keep me updated as best you can.'

Von Schultz knew the meeting was over. He nodded to the count, stood up and walked to the door. He opened the door and turned to look back as the Count spoke one last time.

'I need not remind you Herr Hauptmann that you must be successful in this mission, your family honour depends upon it.'

Von Schultz understood the threat that had just been made and grim faced he opened the door and left the room.

Chapter Seven

Southampton, Hampshire, England - 28 March 1918

Overall, the channel crossing was thankfully quite uneventful; at least we weren't sunk by a mine or a German torpedo or anything. The sea felt a bit rough though and we were all rocked around quite a bit. Actually, more than just quite a bit. The claustrophobic smell of the hot engine diesel oil mixed in with the putrid smell of vomit, which was increasing by the minute didn't make any of us feel any better. The orderlies were fighting a losing battle trying to mop up the vomit which was sloshing around the decks soon after we were out of port, and I knew there wasn't a man on board who wouldn't have given up a year's tobacco ration just to get off that damned ship. I managed to get a shot of morphine from one of the nurses on board and that eased my pain and thankfully my senses quite a bit, along with the obligatory four mugs of rum of course. The nurses were great and kept checking on each of us regularly, lighting cigarettes for anyone who wanted one and generally just trying to keep our spirits up. The constant drone of the engines below us thankfully managed to help drown out the cries of pain and the awful sounds of the gassed soldiers still hacking their lungs up.

Sadly it seemed that the soldier lying next to Jock passed away quietly sometime during the crossing. The nurse who had been sitting with him simply pulled the blanket over his face, sat there for a moment in quiet contemplation, and then walked away, leaving him there. Despite the euphoria of going home, that did put a bit of a dampener on the spirits of the guys around about us. It hit Jock particularly hard; he kept saying that the poor bastard nearly made it back home, but not quite. We had all become quite hardened to death at the front, but when you had some time to think about it, like here on the ship going home, it was all just heartbreaking.

Eventually there came about three loud blasts on the ship's whistle and the sound of the engines changed, slowing down. The rolling of the ship eased off a little and we could see sailors running around the decks. It was obvious even to non-seafaring types like me that we were coming into port. There was a palpable sense of relief on board that we were finally home and reasonably safe. Fritz wouldn't get to us in old Blighty. The whistling, cheering and the singing started up again, although I detected with a little less energy now.

As soon as we finally docked into Southampton harbour the activity on board and around the ship became manic. There were orderlies, nurses and sailors running around everywhere. To me it seemed chaotic, but I think in reality it was probably very highly ordered. They had done it many thousands of times before over the past four years of war and everyone knew what they were supposed to be doing and just got on with it. Apart from the 200 or so wounded soldiers on board of course, we just sat or laid there waiting to see what was going to happen next.

Jock was finally lifted onto a stretcher and taken down the gangplank, just in front of me. The first sight I saw as I came out of the ship's doorway was the low hanging grey clouds and drizzly rain. Good old England's put out its usual welcome for us I thought with a smile. Even with my thick woollen blankets and my tunic wrapped over me, the cold wind and rain still bit deep into my bones as the stretcher bearers carefully picked their way off the ship. I was straining to look around as I was carried down. Along the dockside I could see that there had been constructed rows of huge wooden sheds stretching off into the distance. We were taken from the ship straight into one of these and laid out again in long orderly rows of stretchers. The sheds were just basic sheds, but were well-heated, well-lit and quite comfortable. They certainly kept us out of the biting wind and the rain while we waited for the next bit of our journey.

'Looks like they've done this before eh?' I said to Jock.

'Aye laddie, indeed it does. I wonder how many like us have passed through here over the last four years?'

'Thousands Jock, maybe hundreds of thousands?' I was trying to remember the numbers from my history classes; I wish I'd paid more attention. We laid there for at least an hour, possibly two. I could hear the highly distinctive whooshing and clanging sounds of large steam engines coming from what seemed to be just outside the large wooden shed we were in. There were lots of whistles blowing and much shouting.

Finally, orderlies came in and started hauling the stretchers out of the doors on the opposite side of the shed. We were taken out into a large open holding area and placed down with hundreds of other wounded soldiers on stretchers and the walking wounded were seated on masses of wooden benches. There seemed to be at least fifteen trains sitting waiting next to makeshift wooden platforms with clouds of hot steam belching out from underneath their huge steel wheels. Stretcher bearers were already loading stretchers on board the many carriages up and down the platforms. There were literally hundreds of wounded soldiers and hundreds of stretcher bearers, orderlies, nurses and porters carrying equipment, packing cases and bags; perhaps a thousand people assisting. The cacophony of noise was almost comforting, as we all knew it wasn't shells this time. We were home, in good old England again. I sat up and lit a cigarette for both Jock and me. Despite the melee, looking around I could see that we had quite clearly been placed in areas in accordance with our wounds. The walking wounded were all seated in one area close to us, the stretchers with the gassed and the obviously severely wounded were all placed at the far end, nearest to the trains. Everyone around me and Jock seemed to be fairly lightly wounded stretcher cases.

Eventually the stretcher bearers started lifting the stretchers around about us and leading the walking wounded off. The orderlies came over and checked the labels attached to Jock's and my own Dorothy bags, which we had been clinging onto. We were asked our service numbers, clipboards were checked and ticked, and finally we were off. Jock and I were taken to a train sitting just in front of us and were loaded into one of the white and purplish brown painted carriages which had London and North Western emblems emblazoned on the side. In addition, large red crosses had also been painted along the sides of each carriage.

'Where are we off to now?' I asked one of the orderlies carrying me.

'Dunno mate, I think this one's for Scotland,' he responded.

'Scotland? Why bloody Scotland?' I asked again.

'Dunno mate, mine's not to reason why,' he laughed as they laid my stretcher down and carefully lifted me off and into the comfy looking ward bed inside the carriage. There were two rows of beds, one on either side of the carriage and the beds were in two tiers, one on top of the other. I was in the lower bed and Jock was placed in the bunk directly above me.

'Good luck mate,' said the orderly as they walked away.

'Looks like you're coming home with me then?' Jock laughed down from above.

'Bloody Scotland?' I retorted. 'That's miles away from home.'

'Aye, well never mind laddie, you've got me to keep you company,' laughed Jock again.

The whistles blew and the noise of the steam escaping from the engines grew louder as doors clanged shut up and down the carriages. The sudden screeching and jolting movement of the train told us that we were pulling away from the platform. I laid back and began to think again about home. Where was home now? I lived in Berkhampsted, but that was in 1984. The papers in my pocket stated that I did still live in Berkhampsted, but that was now, in 1918. It was also in a different house, with a wife and child that I had never met and didn't even know. It was so bloody confusing. I tried but I couldn't get my head around any of it.

Sitting up in my bed I could see out of the window reasonably well. The rain ran backwards across the glass in rivulets. The sky was still dull and grey but the hedges, trees and meadows flashing by were green. So very green. Even though in reality I had only been in France for just under a week, the contrast with the stinking grey-black mud of Flanders was striking. God only knows what feelings the other soldiers in the train were experiencing, they had most likely been away in France for three or four years of fighting in that soulless landscape. Of course, technically, as this George Puttnam here in 1918, like them I had also been away in France since August 1915, but I didn't really want to think about that too much. It was too confusing.

The carriage was well-heated, and was becoming a little stuffy with all of the cigarette smoke. I still couldn't get my head around the smoking thing. Even the doctors and nurses were advising you to smoke here in 1918. Complete madness. So I made the grave mistake of pulling open the window next to me a little to get some fresh air. I was instantly covered in choking smoke and dust which was sucked in through the now open window, probably coming directly from the train's funnel.

'Ere lad, shut that window. What are you thinking about?' shouted Jock from above.

'Er sorry mate,' I shouted back as I quickly closed the window again. Having spent years riding around on electric trains how was I to bloody know?

A nurse walked up to me at that point and asked me the obligatory questions - name, rank and serial number. I knew it all off by heart and she wrote the information down on a form on her clipboard.

'Well Corporal, welcome on board ambulance train number 21. I'm nursing Sister Babcock. How are you feeling, do you need any pain relief?' She asked in a very soft and kindly voice. I warmed to her immediately. I thought about it and realised that the pain was beginning to creep up from my leg again. It must have been at least six hours since I had that injection of morphine on board the hospital ship.

'Yes please Sister that would really help. Thank you.'

'That's fine Corporal, I'll get the staff in the dispensary car to organise something for you. If you need anything else just call me or one of my nurses,' she said as she looked up to Jock to start the same conversation all over again with him.

Before long another young nurse with pinned back soft blond hair and a beaming smile came along carrying a small bag and a wooden foot stool. She sat down on the stool next to me and took a very large syringe and a brown glass bottle from her bag.

'Morphine,' she announced, smiling what I thought was just a little too wickedly as she inserted the needle into the top of the bottle and withdrew the liquid. She pulled down the blankets and my pyjama trousers and rolling me over a little she quickly inserted the needle into my right buttock.

'Ouch, that's bloody painful nurse,' I said softly, gritting my teeth.

'Sorry corporal, but it'll help. I'll come back in ten minutes as I've got to change your dressing. The morphine will be working its wonders by then so it should be more comfortable for you.' She stood up, smiled and walked away.

As promised, she was back again in ten minutes with a large enamel cup full of brandy and some new bandages.

'So where exactly are we going nurse?' I asked as she got to work on my dressing.

'Well, first we go into London, Euston station to be exact, and then we go onwards up the North West line towards Glasgow. The train then goes onto a small siding right up to the Merryflats hospital in Govan, which is just beside the Clyde River in Glasgow. I should know, I've done this run four times now.'

'OK, what's Merryflats hospital and why am I going there?'

'It's a recuperation hospital for wounded soldiers, it's very nice and you'll be well looked after there,' she beamed.

'But Glasgow just seems such a long way away?'

'Ah yes but we're short on beds everywhere across the country and usually the less severely wounded get to travel further out. The really bad cases we try and get into hospitals local to the port or into London. It makes sense really doesn't it?'

'Yes I suppose it does make sense,' I agreed. 'Ah well, I guess I'll just have to settle in for a long ride. At least I'm not in France anymore. Got a light?' I asked, as I pulled out my cigarettes.

'Yes of course,' the nurse smiled. I lit two cigarettes and asked the nurse to pass one up to Jock.

'Thanks big-un, much appreciated, aye,' he called down as he took the cigarette from the nurse.

The long journey up to Scotland was again very uneventful and not altogether unpleasant. I had my dressing changed once, drank about five mugs of brandy - to be honest I lost count of those - and smoked at least two packs of cigarettes, a new habit that I just have to stop. The rhythmic clattering of the wheels on the track, combined with the alcohol and the morphine had its effect and I dozed on and off for just about the whole journey. In my waking moments I tried to study the world passing by outside. I noticed a lot more horses in the fields and on the roads and I spotted one or two ancient looking old trucks, which I guessed were probably fairly new, but apart from that the passing countryside didn't look much different from what I was used to. Despite the rain, it was still a very green and pleasant land. It was all quite relaxing and allowed me some time to myself, to think. Everything that had happened to me since waking up in my flat with that creepy soldier and being somehow torn from my armchair and arriving in war torn Flanders has been so vivid, so intense, that I've barely had time to come to terms with my new situation. Suddenly appearing back in 1918 has been like something out of a fiction novel, or a Hollywood movie. It doesn't happen in real life. Only, it has! I tried to make some sense of it all, but couldn't. It made no sense at all. If this was merely a nightmare or an hallucination it has gone on a very long time. I knew though, in my heart of hearts that what I was experiencing was real, very real. This was no imaginary world, the pain and the blood were all too real. The bloody lice seemed real enough too. Before drifting off again I finally came to the conclusion that if I remained here in 1918, I had to somehow find that ghostly soldier. He was my only connection with my other life, the only one who appeared to know what was going on and the only one who might be able to get me back again. Little did I know it then but I wouldn't have too far to search and too long to wait.

Chapter Eight

Merryflats Hospital, Glasgow, Scotland - 29 March 1918

Eventually we reached Glasgow; however we didn't go into Central Station which I was informed the train would normally have done. This was deemed to be a military ambulance train so it was diverted just before the main station and we ended up waiting for what seemed like hours parked up in a railway siding somewhere on the south west side of Glasgow. Finally we steamed back into life again and to the great relief of everyone on board we appeared to be nearing the end of our long journey. After a short ten minute ride there was a great screech of brakes and hissing of hot steam and we came to a theatrical stop right in front of a large and impressive yellow sandstone Victorian building which looked just magnificent in the sunshine that was now starting to break through. Through the carriage windows I could see a number of hospital orderlies, nurses and doctors waiting on the makeshift wooden platform alongside the carriage. The sister and the nurses within the hospital carriage had been packing things away and getting everyone ready for some time before we finally stopped, so as soon as the doors were flung open we were good to go. We all said our tearful goodbyes and had the occasional hug with the nurses whom we had come to know very well over the past twelve hours or so of travelling. Then we were unloaded from the carriages.

I was taken down from the train on a stretcher and carried through a wide open doorway straight into a hospital ward. There were beds lining both walls and only about half of them were occupied. Jock and I were placed next to each other in nice crisp clean beds which were facing a large expanse of windows. Beyond the windows was a wonderful view of well-manicured lawns and bushes leading up to a row of quite stunning Scots pine trees in the middle distance. It was just beautiful, and the sunlight made it all the more wonderful. I laid there looking at our scenic surroundings and despite being horridly wounded, out of time and completely lost with no family or friends, I felt strangely at rest.

Maybe it was just the lack of gunfire and the absence of the constant threat of instant death that installed the peacefulness in me or maybe it was just the morphine, but either way, I felt totally relaxed at that moment.

After all the usual administration and form filling, my new best friend - Nurse Lillian Hampshire from Giffnock - gave us all a mug of rum and a cigarette to help us settle in. We were told that the doctors would be round to examine us within a few hours. There was a lot of banter and requests for updates from the front from many of the lesser wounded guys who were already in the ward when we arrived. They were desperate for any information they could get on the whereabouts and condition of their old units. Although they would obviously be relieved to be away from the dangers of the front, I guess in some way they would be missing their old comrades very much. Let's face it, the trenches had been the only life these men had known for the past few years and they lived, laughed, cried and died with their chums there. This quiet, peaceful world back home was probably still very alien to them. When we arrived we were a very real link to their recent past at the front.

As well as those men asking us for any information we had, there were also the silent ones with the inevitable empty stares. They were the more severely wounded and the shell shocked. Very sad it was to look at them.

All in all we were made to feel very much at home by everyone.

The Matron swept into the ward in a flourish of scarlet shortly after our arrival and introduced herself to the newcomers as Miss Taylor. She was a big buxom and extremely attractive woman of forty-something that obviously had a great deal of character and was certainly going to be no push-over. I was instantly reminded of Sister Marion back in in the hospice in Berkhampsted. I was starting to feel at home again.

As promised, the doctors did their rounds a couple of hours later. A uniformed doctor with a large brown moustache approached my bed accompanied by three other younger doctors in white coats, and the Matron. I must do something about my face I thought as I rubbed my hand over my mouth, I needed to grow one of those moustaches, it was obviously all the rage here. That brought a smile to my face.

The uniformed doctor introduced himself as he looked at my notes. 'Hello there Corporal, I'm Captain Edward Riddle, pleased to meet you and welcome to Glasgow. These gentlemen are my colleagues here. They are the house doctors who will be looking after you whilst you're here at Merryflats hospital,' he said, indicating his colleagues. 'Matron, can you remove the dressing please so that we can see the wound?'

The Matron stepped forward and called over a nurse - who was loitering nearby, obviously ready to be called to action - and asked her to take off the dressing. The nurse carefully removed my bandages. She had to cut away some of the dried blood encrusted bandage close to my skin and that was rather scary. Finally out in the open, my knee felt strangely exposed and vulnerable. It wasn't a nice feeling at all. I could see at least three long deep crimson coloured wounds running down my leg with large stitches still clearly visible. The knee itself looked a very strange shape, quite lumpy and misshapen in fact. I hoped that was still just because of the swelling.

The doctors stepped forward and gathered around my bed.

'As we can see from the notes gentlemen, this patient has had a gunshot wound to the right knee. It seems to have been a clean wound, no infection but it has shattered the knee joint and the knee cap. The surgeons in Rouen have apparently pinned the knee joint together but we'll need an x-ray to see how that looks, then we can make a proper assessment. Matron, can you organise an x-ray please?'

'Certainly Doctor Riddle,' the matron responded whilst jotting a note down on her clipboard.

Captain Riddle turned to face me again. 'We'll get the x-ray done and then we can assess things again Corporal, but for now we'll just keep you comfortable and control the pain. If you feel you need anything just ask one of my team.'

With that he nodded at me, smiled and walked away to the next bed, with his team following on obediently behind.

'They said I'll be out of here and back home in about six or seven weeks,' Jock said loudly as he leaned over and lit two cigarettes, passing one across to me. 'How about you laddie? What did they say?'

'Don't know yet mate, I've got to have an x-ray.'

'Aye well, ne'er mind. Have you heard anything from home yet?' Jock asked.

That stopped me dead in my tracks. Heard anything from home? I hadn't thought of that.

'You mean by letter?' I asked.

'You're a strange 'un and no mistake,' Jock said. 'How else would you hear from home?' he laughed.

'Yes I suppose so,' I said with a forced laugh. 'Er no I haven't actually.'

Aye well never mind laddie, now that we've stopped moving around I'm sure the mail will catch up with us soon enough,' Jock promised. 'I haven't received anything myself in about two months. I'm hoping for a parcel from Ma,' he smiled. 'Aye, I'll probably get a bloody knitted balaclava now I'm back home, which will be about as much use as a chocolate fireguard in here. I hope she sends some ciggies and maybe some whisky?'

'I'll keep my fingers crossed for you Jock,' I laughed.

And sure enough, he was right. It was three days later when Nurse Lillian bounced into the ward, handing out letters from home to the eagerly waiting patients. The excitement in the ward was palpable.

'There are three letters for you Corporal Puttnam and a big parcel for you Jock,' beamed Nurse Lillian as she handed over a little pack of letters tied up with string, addressed in pencil to *Corporal George Puttnam, 88th Division, RFA. On Active Service. France*. I sat there stunned, looking at the letters.

'Well lad, ain't you going to open them and see how the good lady is?' chuckled Jock as he opened his large brown paper wrapped package from his Ma.

'Yes I suppose so,' I answered quietly, unsure as to whether I should even open what felt to me like another man's letters. It seemed like I was prying into someone else's personal life. I sat there for ages just staring at the letters, trying to convince myself that this was me, that this was now my life. Finally I agreed with myself that George Puttnam it seemed was now me for now, for whatever reason, and I had just better get on with it and act like George Puttnam until such time as something else changed or I suddenly found myself back home in my flat again.

I opened the first letter carefully, and began to read the very neat and stylish pencilled writing.

30th December 1917.

My dearest dearest love, George.

I hope this finds you well and in good spirits. Your last letter home said that you were well and that things were not too difficult. I hope that is still holding? Your Christmas wishes to all of us were wonderful to receive and I read your letter to the Children again and again on Christmas Day. Do you remember our wedding on Christmas day my dearest George? I am being truthful if I say that was the most wonderful day of my life.

I don't know where you are now but I read the news journals every day looking for any scrap of news I can find. I hope you are keeping your chin up and know that we are all with you in spirit my dearest George.

The weather here has been grand really. Very mild. I am continuing to work at the smithy and all there is going well and Mr Kempster sends his regards. Mother is continuing to look after the children for us while I am at work and everything is fine there. Mrs Wallace, two doors down has just given birth to her first baby boy and both are doing well. I think that is all the news from home for now. Just to say everyone is still missing you terribly my love, and no more so than me, young Evelyn who talks about you all the time and of course baby Daisy who has not met you yet. She still has that pleasure to come. Please please take good care of yourself and come home to us safely my love.

Best wishes for the New Year my darling. Let's hope and pray that 1918 will be a better year for all of us and that you will be home by next Christmas?

Please write soon.

Wishing you all of our love and you are always in our prayers.

Your adoring wife, Violet.

'Wow,' I whispered under my breath. It was short, simple but it spoke volumes. It seemed that I had a loving wife and two children, not just the one I thought I had. A real family! I wiped a tear from my eye and opened the next envelope, reading it carefully. It was fairly similar in content, providing me with snippets of news from home, urging me to keep my chin up and reminding me of the love my family had for me. The last, most recent letter had more of a sense of distress about it though.

14th March 1918.

To my dearest love, George.

I hope this finds you well and with your spirits as high as they can be. I haven't heard from you since last month and I am being honest if I say that we are all terribly worried.

I don't know where you are or what is happening but I am hoping and praying that all is well with you and that you are safe. We all are. Your mother sends all of her love. The flu is hitting everyone hard here and it has claimed several people in the village, we are all worried about that. Thankfully so far Evelyn, Daisy and I have avoided catching it as have both of our families. I do not know how long that will last? I am doing my best to keep us safe and avoiding anyone who I think may have contracted the flu.

Please please do find the time to write to us George. Your news means so much to all of us, just a few words to hear that you are safe keeps us all going and knowing that you will be home with us again one day makes life worth living.

Please please look after yourself.

Wishing you all our love, as always. You are in our prayers.

Your adoring wife, Violet, Evelyn and Daisy

Choking back the tears I read the letter over and over again. I knew that I needed to put pen to paper and write back, there and then. There was no other George to write back, I don't know why and I don't know how, but there was only me, and this family needed something, from George. So it was down to me now. I called the nurse over and asked for some paper, a pen and an envelope. The nurse brought back three sheets of writing paper, one small envelope and a sharp pencil. I hadn't used a pencil since my primary school days, but what the heck, it would do. I laid out the paper on my tray and was poised with my pencil, but I hesitated. I was unsure what to write. I had no idea what any of my previous letters had been like or what I had written, or how I even spoke to Violet. Eventually I decided that I would just go with it and let my heart do the talking. I had read enough about the two world wars to know that my letter would most likely be censored before it was finally received by Violet, so I figured that it was probably best that I didn't mention too many specific details. I had read that many soldiers in World War 1 had devised a code system for writing home before they left for the front so that they could avoid the censor and let their wives and families know where they were, but obviously if the previous George had done that, I had no knowledge of it, or if I was indeed that George, then I had no memory of it. That thought stopped me dead. Was I in fact really that George? Violet's George? And had I just lost my memory? Mmmmm, I figured I'd have to give that one some more thought, but for now I had a letter to write.

1st April 1918.

To my dearest loves, Violet, Evelyn and Daisy,

I hope this letter finds you all well and in good spirits. I must apologise for not writing sooner. We have been very busy and up to our eyes in it lately and it has been difficult to find the time to sit down and write. I have some news for you my love. If you haven't been notified already, I have been wounded in my right leg and I am now back in old Blighty, safe and sound. Don't worry about me though, I am fine and well on the mend. Unfortunately I am rather further north than Berkhampsted as I am now in Scotland, recuperating in a lovely scenic hospital in a place called Govan, it's near Glasgow. I hope everything is going well at home?

I will write again soon and let you know my progress. Hopefully I will be fit enough to be released soon. I am so looking forward to coming home and seeing you all again.

Please write again soon.

All my love,

George xx

I tried to write the letter in what I thought might be the style of someone from 1918, but it's very difficult and I'm not sure if I succeeded or not. The times had changed so much, the culture, the language, everything. It was almost like a foreign country to me. Anyway, I thought it best to keep the letter short and concise, and hopefully I had managed to put nothing in there the censors wouldn't like, or perhaps more importantly, that Violet wouldn't pick up as extremely unusual. I didn't want to risk upsetting her.

I was also very worried about the flu pandemic Violet mentioned which was sweeping the world at the moment. From memory I knew that it came in two waves between 1918 and

1920, with the second wave at the end of 1918 going into 1919 being the deadliest. I also knew that it was responsible for more deaths in one year than the Black Death caused over the course of a century. Some 50 to 100 million people worldwide were killed over a 24 month period, that was around 5% of the world's population which made it one of the deadliest natural disasters in human history. Much worse than the actual war itself. I remember learning that it was an unusual virus in that it caused a severe overreaction of the body's immune system which meant that young fit adults were worst hit and the symptoms were terrifying, often with severe bleeding from the nose, ears and stomach. Death usually followed soon afterwards. Weaker, older people and the very young were much less affected.

I remembered from school that the flu virus was named the Spanish Flu at the time but that only came about because the reporting of deaths from the flu was suppressed by the censors in those countries at war with each other so that it didn't lower the morale of the soldiers in the trenches and the people back home any further. Spain wasn't at war with anyone so they openly reported the full extent of the flu pandemic in their country, which gave the misleading impression that the flu was more severe in Spain than anywhere else. I knew that the pandemic was thought to have been exacerbated by the conditions of the war and I was interested to learn that in civilian life natural selection favours a mild strain of virus as people with really bad cases of flu usually go home and stay in bed while people with mild cases continue on as normal, thereby spreading the mild strain around whilst the virulent strain is isolated. Natural immunities are then built up in the local population. But in the trenches on the western front this situation was totally reversed. Soldiers with the mild cases stayed where they were, in the trenches, whilst the severely ill soldiers were sent back on crowded ambulance trains to crowded field hospitals and then onto crowded troop ships and into crowded hospitals back at home. The vast movement of soldiers around the world at that time ensured the fast global spread of the virulent flu strain. It was a worrying time and I was really worried for Violet and if I'm honest, probably myself too now that I thought about it.

I listened to the various coughs and sneezes around the ward with renewed interest. Something else to worry about.

I addressed the envelope using the address in my pay book and handed it back to the nurse, unsealed. Done. First contact made with my family, whoever they were, and all I had to worry about now was actually meeting them in the flesh. I wondered, with not a little trepidation, what that would be like.

The next few weeks passed by very slowly, and these rolled into months. There was a daily routine of breakfast, followed by a wash, the doctor's rounds, lunch, and an afternoon resting in the garden when the weather allowed, which was surprisingly often given that we were in Scotland. Then came dinner and lights out at 9.30 pm. The nurses were wonderful and we all grew very attached to each other. Fortunately most of the soldier's wounds were not life threatening and it was on the whole a fairly happy ward, but we did have one or two more severe cases and there were two deaths on the ward during my time there. That was very sad for all of us, staff and patients alike, and there were many tears all round.

I never grew tired of the stories from the other patients and the nursing staff. Their tales were truly amazing, funny, sad, tear jerking and occasionally shocking - often all in one go. One thing that was taboo though were our war experiences. The talk was usually about family, past lives and future plans, no one really dwelt on the war apart from when new patients arrived and there was a renewed clamour for information from the front. The nightmares and the continual screams in the still of the night were memory enough for most of the men. No one needed to share and relive their horrors in the daytime, for now anyway. Perhaps they never would.

The food was fair enough. Lots of potatoes, vegetables and the occasional fatty piece of meat. We had black and white pudding and an amazing square Lorne sausage with our breakfasts and we even had haggis, neaps and tatties for dinner on more than one occasion. It was an acquired taste but I really grew to like the spicy flavours of the haggis, a truly unique Scottish dish, real exotic dining. But best of all, the food was hot. The food at the front was always, perhaps understandably, stone cold.

Jock left us and went home sometime at the end of August. We dispensed with the handshakes and went straight for the big manly hug as he left. Jock and I had become the best of friends during our short time together and as we swapped home addresses we promised to stay in touch. He joked that I would have to come up and visit him as it might be some time before he would be able to sit in a train again for 12 hours as he no longer had an arse. We both laughed at that. I sincerely hoped we would stay in touch, I certainly intended to try - as long as I remained in 1918 that was.

I had my x-ray. I didn't even know that x-rays had been invented in 1918. I wish I had access to that new internet; I would have looked that one up. The equipment used looked a bit Victorian but it was probably state-of-the-art here in 1918 and it obviously worked well enough. The x-ray confirmed what the doctors already thought, that I had received a gunshot wound through my right knee, shattering the joint, the ligaments and the knee cap itself. The surgeons in Rouen had indeed inserted a couple of metal plates into my leg and bolted the lot together. This all seemed to have healed well enough but I no longer had any ability to bend my leg at the knee joint. In fact I no longer had a knee joint. Looking on the bright side, at least I hadn't lost my leg I suppose.

The doctors, nurses and a physiotherapist worked on me for many weeks to get me standing and walking, first with the aid of crutches and then by early September I was walking just with the aid of a stick. Everyone said it was remarkable progress.

Early in October I had an interview with Captain Riddle and he got me to answer a whole load of questions about my home life and my family details, most of which I hoped I had answered correctly. The bits I had no idea on I just made up. He then got me to walk up and down in front of him with my stick. I managed this well enough and was really quite pleased with myself. The Captain then asked me to sit down and I watched him as he ticked off boxes on the paperwork in front of him. After what seemed like ages, he cleared his throat and solemnly informed me that as I had no lasting disability from the injury sustained whilst on active service he would reject any application for a war pension. As I hadn't applied for a war pension - whatever that was anyway - I wasn't worried too much, but I did question his comment regarding the fact that I had no permanent disability. I merely suggested to the Doctor that the complete loss of my knee joint surely must be considered a permanent injury, as there was no chance of it ever fixing itself or going back to how it used to be. Captain Riddle almost had an apoplectic fit. His face went red, his eyes bulged and he stood up immediately and shoving some papers in my hand he ordered me out of his office, mumbling something about 'the insolence of the man'. I was actually too astonished to say anything at the time, and I didn't really attach too much importance to it then, but as it turned out, perhaps I should have done. If that's how they dealt with the men who had been serving at the front for years, risking life and limb, and then returned injured, then I wasn't impressed at all.

I limped back to my bed and read through the papers. It was all a bit confusing. One was headed Army Form B178 and stamped *'For DISPERSAL under Authority WO Letter 122/834 (mob 26) - Dispersal Hospital, Stobhill Glasgow.* The paperwork stated clearly that *this soldier has suffered no impairment in health since his entry into the services.* That's bloody rich I thought, no impairment in health? Good grief. Anyway, it looked like I was being dispersed back to my barracks in Woolwich, London. At least that was a bit closer to home. Whatever home was, it would be good to go and find out. I didn't seem to have much else to do.

The next morning the nurse delivered my tunic, neatly cleaned and pressed, a cleaned pair of second hand trousers, a pair of second hand boots, thankfully in my size, new long johns and thick woollen socks. I put my old but clean uniform on, with some difficulty, and had to get an orderly to tie up my boot laces. I hoped Velcro would be invented soon as I could see tying up laces without bending my leg was going to be an ongoing challenge. I packed everything I owned - which wasn't much - into a small army back pack they had given me and sat on the bed, waiting for whatever was to come next.

Chapter Nine

Colmworth, Bedfordshire, England - 6 September 1918

Hauptmann Claus Von Schultz jumped down from the rear of the British army truck that he had been travelling in and flexed his massive frame. He and the other three German officers stood there in the relatively warm late summer sun looking around them whilst the single British soldier guarding them locked the tailgate of the truck back into position and then gave a bang onto the side of the truck to notify the driver he could move on.

Von Schultz looked around the wire perimeter fence of the compound and smiled. The single wire fence that separated them from the rolling green fields beyond was about three metres high with one coil of barbed wire running along the top. He could see only about four British Tommys with Lee Enfield rifles guarding the perimeter of the camp and one guard at the gate. Security wasn't tight here he thought to himself. There were a number of other prisoners milling around the yard in various German uniforms, all officer ranks. They were watching the newcomers with interest.

'All right you lot, line up over 'ere,' shouted the guard, indicating a space directly in front of a wooden reception hut with his rifle. The four dusty, dirty and tired German officers dutifully lined up as ordered. At that point a young British officer, resplendent in his newly pressed uniform and highly polished brown boots and Sam Browne belt, stepped out of the reception hut doorway and strode over to stand directly in front of the four German officers. Tucking his brown leather baton under his arm he addressed the prisoners.

'Good afternoon gentlemen. Welcome to Duck's Cross Camp which will be your home for the foreseeable future. My name is Lieutenant Croft and I am the officer in charge here.'

Only a lieutenant? Von Schultz thought. The British didn't seem to be taking this seriously he pondered. Maybe they mistakenly thought the Germans were only too pleased to be out of the war and safe and had no intention of escaping?

'We are all officers and gentlemen here,' the lieutenant droned on in English, having no mind as to whether the prisoners could even understand him or not. 'As long as you respect us we will afford you the same respect in return. We want no funny business here gentlemen, and no attempts at escaping. If you try to escape we will shoot you, make no mistake about that,' he warned. 'If you play the game we will all get along just fine.' He beamed from under his large brown moustache.

'Carry on Sergeant,' he said loudly to the British soldier with the three stripes on his arm standing just behind him. And with those few words, Lieutenant Croft walked smartly back into the wooden hut, closing the door firmly behind him.

'Right then, you 'eard the officer!' bawled the sergeant. 'No funny business and we'll get along just fine. Simms, you take these 'ere gentlemen over to block five and get them acquainted with their new 'omes,' he said, indicating to the single guard who had travelled in the truck with the prisoners.

The guard walked over to the line of prisoners and pointed over to one of the huts in the far corner of the yard.

'Follow me,' he said, walking off with his rifle now slung over his shoulder.

Von Schultz smiled broadly again. This just gets better and better he thought.

As they entered the darkness of the hut the guard indicated four neatly made up empty bunk beds just next to the door.

'These are yours,' he said, before turning and walking straight back out of the door again.

Von Schultz and his three fellow prisoners threw their bags down onto a bunk each just as they were approached by three other officer inmates who had been standing chatting at the rear of the hut.

'Welcome to your new home,' said the taller of the officers in a thick Prussian accent. He was dressed in a German Kaiserliche Marine uniform with full regalia. 'I am Kapitan Erich Gröner and I am the German officer in charge here at Duck's Cross Camp,' he said, holding out his hand to shake hands with each of the newcomers. They each shook hands with him except for Von Schultz, who stood with his own hands clasped firmly behind his back.

Kapitan Gröner stared with obvious annoyance at Von Schultz for a second or two before carrying on.

'I have been here since Jutland in 1916. The British have treated us as gentlemen and we have reciprocated accordingly. Although security is light here, we as officers have given our word that we will not attempt to escape or cause any undue trouble for our captors. Great Britain is an island and even if we were to escape this camp we would be unlikely to manage safely the journey to the coast, across the channel and through the British lines in northern France, back to our homeland. We have to be realistic. If we want to survive and see our families again, we have to play the game with the British. Remember, we have already played our part in this Great War with honour. There is nothing to be ashamed of. Please make yourselves at home here gentlemen and if you need anything just ask. I will talk with each of you later today once you have settled in. Thank you.'

With that the Kapitan and his fellow officers turned and left the new-comers alone in the hut.

'What a load of bullshit,' growled Von Schultz to the other three prisoners. 'They are traitors, the lot of them. It is our duty to escape and rejoin the war effort, for our Kaiser and fatherland.'

'But what's the point? The Kapitan is right. We can't go anywhere so we might as well make life comfortable for ourselves,' said a young Oberleutnant.

Von Schultz grabbed the young officer by his throat, squeezing his windpipe violently.

'We are German officers and we are fighting a war, a war we are eventually going to win.' Von Schultz snarled at the young Oberleutnant before throwing him back onto a bunk.

'Now leave me alone, I have a job to do and plans to make,' Von Schultz said as he walked out and slammed the door behind him.

Chapter Ten

Going Home - 10 October 1918

The train journey back to London was thankfully uneventful, if not a little uncomfortable. The imposing black painted London and North Western Railway steam locomotive was surprisingly fast; the conductor had already boasted that we would be travelling at speeds of up to 90 miles per hour and that we would be in London within ten and a half hours. I would have preferred to have jumped on the British Airways shuttle out of Glasgow and be in Heathrow in just under an hour, but that wasn't going to happen for another 50 years yet. I was of course stuck down in cattle class with wooden seats and no suspension. The rattling and banging of the carriage was jarring my leg badly so there was not much opportunity for sleeping. I did however pass the time studying the differences in the local landscape as we flashed by and I found that I thoroughly enjoyed people-watching my fellow passengers. There were a number of soldiers travelling, presumably making their way back to their barracks like me or perhaps en-route to the front. I hoped not. I enjoyed looking at the clothing of the various ladies on board too. Many wore much repaired and tired looking coats and dresses. Britain had been at war for a long time and it showed. I did however get many sympathetic smiles from many of the ladies and a good pat on the shoulder from a number of the male passengers and the other soldiers. That made me feel really quite proud, even though I personally hadn't actually done any real fighting, although to be fair, George Puttnam almost certainly had.

I think I must have smoked at least two packets of Woodbines on my way down to London and at times the smog inside the carriage was un-breathable. I had learned my lesson last time though, there was little point in opening a window.

I finally arrived at Euston Station in London and then had to make my own way across the city to the Royal Field Artillery barracks in Woolwich. I had been given a military on-service pass at the hospital so I could fortunately go anywhere free with that, which made life a bit easier as I had no idea how to buy a ticket in this time or any idea of the cost, and there were no ticket machines that I could see either. I did have a few shillings on me that the hospital had provided on my discharge, courtesy of the war office, so I had some funds. I wasn't in any particular hurry so I just took my time, enjoying looking at the city sights from a time over forty years before I was born.

I wasn't sure as to what I should expect when I got to the barracks. I had no formal military training, or at least if I did have it was now forgotten, so I was worried about how I would fit back in. I needn't have worried though. As soon as I arrived at the Woolwich barracks I was taken straight from the guard house, walking past the historic Napoleonic cannons and under the imposing white arches into the huge regimental building where I was told to wait in a large reception area. I was eventually asked by an orderly to follow him and he took me up the sweeping staircase to a small office on the first floor. Inside was a tired looking young officer sitting behind a large mahogany desk. He stood up as I came in and held out his hand.

'Good afternoon Corporal. It's nice to see you. I hope your journey hasn't been too traumatic? I'm Lieutenant Sidney White,' he said whilst shaking my hand vigorously. 'Please sit down.'

I did as he asked, leaning my walking stick carefully against my chair and gingerly sitting down.

'Well Corporal,' he began whilst flicking through some papers in front of him. 'Nearly three years at the front. I see you've seen lots of action too eh?'

'Er yes, I guess so,' I stammered.

'Now now, don't be modest,' he said, smiling broadly. 'You've done your bit and we're proud of you.'

'Thank you,' I said, not knowing what else to say.

'How is the wound Corporal?'

'Not too bad sir, I can get around now with my stick.'

'Good, good. Well done. Now let's sort your papers. I'm sure you don't want to be hanging around here for too long do you?'

'No sir,' I responded, still not knowing what was going on or what else to say.

'This here form I'm signing now is form B179B which states your disability and transfers you to the military reserve with immediate effect.'

The Lieutenant looked up and smiled at me, clearly expecting some kind of response.

'Er, what exactly does that mean sir?'

'It means Corporal, that you can go straight home now. Well at least until we realise we can't win this war on our own and we need you back again,' he said, beaming from ear to ear as he handed over the signed papers to me.

'Here's a chitty for the remaining pay that we owe you. Please collect that at the cash desk on the ground floor on your way out. You'll need your pay book as well for that. Keep your uniform safe and look after it at home, remember, you are in the reserve now. We may still need you again one day. Thank you for your excellent service corporal and well done,' he said, the short meeting obviously now finished. I stood up and we both shook hands. I picked up my walking stick and headed slowly out of the door and down to the pay office.

Within three hours I was back inside Woolwich Arsenal station again, looking for the train back to Charing Cross, and then onto the Hampstead tube line to Euston where I could catch the train to Berkhampsted - or at least I hoped I could.

Moving around the stations, especially the underground was made difficult and slow because of my disability, but there were no shortages of good Samaritans willing to assist me in any way they could. After the horrors of the Somme, my faith in human kind was restored somewhat. People here appeared to be extremely grateful for the sacrifices their soldiers had made, and it showed. Other soldiers either nodded at me or saluted and I had to keep remembering to salute any officers I met. Most of the men

I saw were dressed in a uniform of some sort and many of the women were dressed in working clothes and various uniforms too. I noticed that the buses and trains were all being run by women, and many of the porters on the station were also women. Whilst that seemed quite acceptable to me, I knew that in this time that had been a complete change to the culture and everyone was still trying to come to terms with it. Before the war women had not been allowed to work at all after they married and they still did not have the vote yet. The war had changed many things in society, and whilst some of the major gains women had made during the war would be lost when the men returned, things would never again fully return to the old ways of the Edwardian era. Women still had a long way to go to achieve full equality, and they still didn't have it in my time in 1984, but this was the start, it was the passing of the old era into the modern age, and I was actually here to witness it. I found it hard to believe really.

Eventually I arrived on the platform at Euston Station and boarded the train to Berkhampsted. This time I sat in a second class carriage. My free pass only entitled me to third class travel, but after all I had been through I felt I deserved it, so I decided to make my protest and I just sat there. I didn't think anyone would actually throw me out, and I was happily proved right. Maybe I should have gone for First Class.

After about an hour we were passing through Boxmoor station, next stop Berkhampsted. My stomach was starting to knot itself nicely.

The platform on Berkhampsted station was very quiet when I arrived in the warm early evening. One or two other people got off the train with me and hurried off the platform. The conductor blew his whistle, waved his flag and jumped back on the train again as it pulled out of the station amidst great clouds of steam. Steam locomotives are such beautiful things I thought to myself, much more dramatic than electric trains. I slung my backpack over my shoulder and started to follow the other people out of the station, whistling the tune to Goody Two Shoes by Adam Ant.

'Well bless my soul, if it isn't George, George Puttnam!' shouted a short man in a long black greatcoat with shiny brass buttons down the front. He had an official looking black cap perched firmly on his head and a sharply waxed moustache stuck under his nose. He was walking towards me with his hand outstretched, obviously wanting to shake mine. As he reached me he grabbed my hand and started to pump it up and down as his other hand slapped me hard on the shoulder.

'How the devil are you George? I had no idea you were coming home. Does Violet know?' He asked.

'Em, no I don't think she does, it's a sort of surprise,' I blurted. I didn't have a clue who he was and I could see this was going to be a recurring problem for me.

'You need anything George, anything at all you just let old Percy know, I'm always down 'ere at the station,' he said, smiling and whacking me on the shoulder again as I hurriedly limped off, thanking him profusely.

'Give my love to that wonderful young lady of yours,' he shouted after me as I left the platform through the little wooden gate and wandered out to the front of the station. It was a lovely autumn evening, the sun was just starting to go down and the air was fresh, but not too cold yet. I left my greatcoat folded up in my back pack; I wouldn't need that just yet. I pulled out a woodbine from my tunic pocket and lit it, inhaling the damaging smoke deep into my lungs. No coughing this time. I must stop this soon I promised myself, yet again. I looked to the left, up the lane that took you under the railway and round to Berkhampsted castle. It was much narrower than in my time, and noticeably completely bereft of cars. A horse and cart piled up with hay came rumbling along from the other direction, followed by a vintage looking van which seemed to be going slower than the horse.

My pay-book stated that my home was at number nine George Street. I wasn't exactly sure where that was but I had an idea it might be over by the canal somewhere, close to the Boat Inn where I had often had a pint or two while sitting in the beer garden. I used to love watching the barges float serenely up and down the Grand Union canal, I always found that quite relaxing. I was usually on my own of course, but it was quite pleasant all the same. With that in mind I turned right and walked up the lane in that direction.

Following Station Road to the end I turned right onto Ravens Lane and there in front of me was The Boat Inn pub. Different from how I remembered it, but not that much different. Gone were the trendy beer garden awnings and the gastro pub menus outside, but the building itself was definitely the same. Just past the pub on the left was George Street. My street, apparently.

I had the strongest urge to carry straight on down Ravens Lane, turn right onto the High Street and then on up to my flat above the betting shop. But I knew deep down that there would be no betting shop, and the flat above, if indeed it even existed, would almost certainly be occupied by someone else. I had to accept this was 1918 and not 1984. This was my home now; there was nowhere else to go, so I might as well get on with it. Besides, I knew Violet was there, waiting for me. I was scared for sure and my stomach was churning even faster now, but also I was very intrigued to meet her. I wondered then for the first time if perhaps she would realise I wasn't her George. What would I do then? I guessed I would just have to face that if it came to it I thought.

I stood at the top of George Street looking down. From the numbers I could see I estimated that number nine would be just a little way down on the left. Nervously I pulled another cigarette out of my packet and lit it up, just to calm me down I told myself. I stood there for what seemed like an age, just looking down the street as the shadows of the houses lengthened across the road in the setting sun. Resolving myself, I stubbed out my cigarette under my boot and strode purposefully down the street towards the house.

As I came to it I could see that number nine George Street was a narrow Victorian terrace house with a small bay window and a shiny red front door. I thought it looked very neat and tidy and really quite quaint. I swung open the small, well-oiled wrought iron front gate and walked the three or four steps up to the red tiled doorstep. Taking a deep breath I lifted the highly polished brass door knocker and rapped the door three times.

Hardly daring to breathe I stood there waiting, forcing my legs to stop quivering and trying my best to hold my stomach in place. I actually felt quite sick; my nerves were getting the better of me.

After a few minutes I heard someone walking down the hallway inside and saw a shadow appear behind the front door's frosted window pane. I heard a bolt being slid back and a key being turned from inside. The door opened slowly.

This was it!

'Hello who's there?' came the soft voice from behind the door.

The door opened fully and there in front of me stood the most beautiful looking girl I have ever seen. Long auburn hair, red full lips, and the most striking deep green eyes which were staring unblinking up at me.

'George,' she whispered.

'George!' Louder this time.

'GEORGE!' She screamed as she hurled herself at me, wrapping her arms around me and weeping pitifully into my chest. Behind her I saw a little girl come running down the hallway towards us, followed closely by an almost identical but even smaller girl.

'Daddy daddy!' shouted the first little girl as she reached me and flung her arms around my legs. The other little girl, whom I assumed was little Daisy just stood there in the hallway staring at us.

'George, I can't believe it's really you, you're home?' wept Violet, wiping her wet nose against the rough wool of my tunic.

I put my arms around her tiny waist. In fact I couldn't believe my luck. This beautiful young woman hugging me and looking like she never intended letting go of me ever again. Never in my wildest dreams could I have imagined this. We must have stood there like that for five minutes at least, neither one of us wanting to let go, to break the moment. I was just enjoying being cuddled like that. It had been a long time since anyone had ever wanted to cuddle me. Finally young Daisy walked up to me, grabbed one of my hands and tugged.

'Daddy, come see my dolly,' she said and pulled harder. Violet looked down at her and rubbing the top of Daisy's head she grabbed my other hand and both of them pulled me into the hallway, with Evelyn still attached to my legs. The tears were still streaming down Violet's face and I noticed then that they were running freely down my own too.

'Come Evelyn, Daisy, let's get Daddy into the front parlour,' said Violet as she pulled me into the hallway, kicking the front door shut behind us. We turned left into the first doorway we came to. It was a small front room which had a red and brown tapestry sofa along one wall and two high backed leather armchairs either side of the fireplace. There was a small table, with a white lace tablecloth over it, positioned in the bay window. It was obvious that this room was rarely used and was probably kept for special occasions. It smelled a little stale.

'Daisy you go and get your dolly to show daddy,' Violet said. As Daisy ran out of the door, Violet turned to me again and flung her arms around my neck pulling my face down towards hers. Her wet lips found mine and we held each other tightly as our lips and tongues caressed. Even through the thick woollen material of my uniform I could feel Violet's ample breasts pushing against my torso and it was all starting to have a serious effect on me. Violet pushed her hips against mine and leaned back a little, looking into my eyes.

'Mmmmm George, I think it might be early to bed tonight?' she beamed.

'Daddy Daddy, see my dolly!' shouted Daisy as she hurtled back into the room holding out a soft doll in a frilly white wedding dress. 'Grandma made it for me.'

Unwilling to let go of Violet, I squatted down to examine the doll whilst still holding one of Violet's hands.

'Wow that's lovely,' I said cooing over her doll. 'What's her name?'

'Amy Louise, after Grandma,' she said proudly.

I finally let go of Violet's hand and put my arm around Evelyn who had been waiting patiently. Evelyn put her arms around my neck and hugged me close.

'Evelyn has missed you my darling,' said Violet. 'We all have, so much,' and with that she started to cry again. Sob would be a better description, she was a wreck.

'I'm so sorry my love, it's just that I never really thought I would ever see you again. I've been waiting for the knock at the door and that awful telegram for three years now, like the one Mrs Deacon received only last week.'

'I know my love, but I'm home again now and everything is going to be all right,' I said, not quite believing it fully. I still had no idea when this was all going to end and if I would suddenly find myself back in my old flat in 1984. I think I was even starting to hope that I would never go back, I just wanted this moment to go on forever.

'Please sit down my darling,' Violet said, indicating that I should sit on the sofa. 'How are you? How is your wound? We received your letters from Scotland and we were terrified, thinking that you had lost your leg. Is it painful my love?'

'No not too bad,' I said as I tried to lower myself down onto the sofa with as much dignity as I could muster. As soon as I sat down Evelyn dived in next to me and Daisy started to climb up onto my lap.

'Stop it Daisy, watch out for your poor Daddy's leg,' Violet warned.

'It's OK my love,' I laughed as I lifted Daisy up onto my good side. I patted the seat next to me and Violet came and sat down, very close. I was very aware of the heat of her thigh against mine. I was loving this, it was better than winning the football pools. The next hour or so was just a blur. We sat there chatting, hugging and crying in equal measures and I felt like I had been with these three people all of my life. It was absolutely wonderful. Obviously Violet wanted to know what my life had been like at the front. As I had actually only experienced a few days of it I just told her I didn't really want to talk about it right now. I think she accepted that. I was however able to tell her all about my adventures in getting back from the front, the ambulances, the field hospitals, the train journeys, the channel crossing and my time in Scotland. Violet just sat there holding my hand, awestruck at my adventures. Violet also filled me in on the goings on in our community back here in Berkhampsted. Of course I didn't know any of the people that she was telling me about, but I played along, hopefully convincingly.

Eventually we all went through into the little living room in the middle of the house, where a small fire was burning in the grate. There was a large wooden dining table in the centre of the room and a few smaller armchairs in each of the corners. It was a very cosy little room and it seemed to be the room that we lived in most of the time. The door at the back of the living room led out into the long thin kitchen area. I followed Violet down the one step into the kitchen, leaving the girls to play in the family room. The kitchen was very warm, heated by the iron cooking range in the alcove along the back wall. On the range was a large pot of something bubbling away.

'Beef stew and dumplings,' Violet explained when she saw me looking at the pot. She lifted the hot lid with a cloth in her hand and gave the stew a stir. 'Although there's not much beef in here,' she said apologetically. 'Things have been tough lately.'

I could tell from the multiple repairs in the pretty floral dress Violet was wearing that we obviously weren't exactly flush with money. I didn't mind, I thought she looked stunning.

I wanted to ask questions such as: Do we own this house? What do we live on? Where do I work? Do I have any other clothes? Where is the toilet? But I held back. I didn't want to freak her out just yet. Mind you, I knew I would have to find the toilet soon.

That little problem was soon resolved.

'Mummy, need pee pee mummy,' shouted Daisy as she ran into the kitchen.

'Be a love and take Daisy to the toilet would you my darling?' said Violet as she picked up some dishes and carried them into the living room.

That could have been a problem but I was saved by Daisy pulling me towards the back door, just off the kitchen. We went outside into a very small courtyard that runs alongside the kitchen. Daisy pulled me round to the back wall of the kitchen where there was an old wooden door which had a six inch gap at the top and bottom. It looked suspiciously like a toilet door I thought. Daisy waited while I lifted the latch and opened the door and then she ran in. Inside was an old toilet on a little tiled pedestal with a large metal flush tank above and a long chain hanging down. Daisy pulled her underwear down and waited for me to lift her onto the toilet. She sat there and smiled at me while she tore off two or three sheets of a strange waxy toilet paper from the roll hanging on the wall. The paper had IZAL written across it in green and it was very shiny and hard. I certainly wasn't looking forward to using that when I needed to do a number two! When Daisy had finished I let her run back to the kitchen while I emptied my bursting bladder.

'Bloody hell, that's cold out there now,' I said, rubbing my hands together as I walked back into the kitchen.

'Now now George, that's no language to use in the house, you're not in the trenches now you know!' Violet said firmly as she slapped me playfully on the arm. I had to think what I had said for a minute. Bloody hell? Was that it? That wasn't swearing. My, how times had changed. If Violet had scolded me over the use of bloody hell, I knew I'd have to think carefully about the language I was using from here on in, I had much worse than that in my usual daily vocabulary.

'Let's have dinner now. George, girls, I think we're all set,' said Violet, ushering us all to the table in the living room which was now laid with a floral tablecloth, four white bowls, four spoons and a large pot of stew with chunks of bread in the centre of the table.

'Mmmm looks lovely,' I commented as we all sat down, Violet at one end of the table, me at the other and the girls on either side. Violet dished out the steaming hot stew to each of us and I picked up my spoon ready to plunge it into the bowl in front of me when I saw Violet giving me a frown from the other end of the table. I sat there motionless looking at her.

'Where are your manners George? Have you forgotten everything since you've been at the front? You can say grace before we start.'

Gulp. Awkward moment. I had no idea how to say grace.

'Em I'm a bit out of practice my love, would you say it please?' I stammered. Violet said a few words thanking God or someone for the food and then everyone tucked in. There were certainly a few things I was going to have to get used to in this strange 1918 world. The food was plain and wholesome and I was starving hungry so it went down a treat. Violet had done wonders with what little food we obviously had. I was amazed at her abilities and how she had held everything together on her own, with two young children to care for over the past three and a half years. The shortages caused by the war and the lack of money, combined with the emotional strain of waiting every day to hear that her husband had been killed, and also having to take on a new job at the smithy at the same time must have put an enormous strain on her. I just sat there and stared at her admiringly while she ate. What a woman. They all were.

After dinner Violet and I went into the kitchen and washed up. I took a large pan of boiling water which Violet had previously put on the range and took it over to the big white sink in front of the kitchen window. I poured it into the sink and used that to wash the dishes while Violet dried.

'I can't believe you are finally home my darling, all those years of worrying and dreading the post boy coming are at an end. I love you so much you know,' she said, her eyes smiling at me as the tears streamed down both cheeks. I put the dishcloth down, wiped my hands on my trousers and put my arms around her again.

'I love you too Violet,' I said. And I meant it. I had never said that to anyone else before, but it felt perfectly natural now. In the short time I had been with Violet I truly believed I had fallen deeply in love with her. We stood there hugging and kissing again until we were interrupted by several loud coughs. Evelyn was standing in the kitchen doorway holding a book.

'OK my darling; we're just coming to read your books with you. Would you like Daddy to read to you tonight?' offered Violet.

'Yes please Daddy,' said Evelyn.

We quickly finished up in the kitchen and I went and sat in one of the cosy armchairs in the living room while the girls made themselves comfortable around me on cushions which had been spread on the floor. The girls gave me their books and I read each in turn. Violet brought in a large dark bottle and a glass for me. She poured out the thick dark liquid and smiled at me.

'I kept this for you coming home my love,' she beamed, handing me the glass. The beer was thick and warm and unlike anything I had ever tasted before, but not unpleasant. We sat there for over an hour with Violet and me taking turns to read stories. It was truly wonderful and fair to say it was the happiest moment in my life so far.

'Time for bed girls,' Violet said at last. Violet took the girls outside to the toilet and then we all trooped up the stairs and I did my best to help Violet get the girls ready and into bed. I was probably more of a hindrance than a help and Violet said it had taken twice as long tonight, but she didn't seem to mind.

Violet and I went back downstairs and we spent two wonderful hours chatting about everything and nothing while I finished my second beer and Violet had a glass of port. The flickering light from the wall gas lamps made the room feel very cosy, and helped to stir my romantic feelings. I hoped they were doing the same with Violet. I managed to steer most of the conversation around to her life, tiptoeing around and trying to find out important things without letting on I knew nothing about her. For instance, asking her how her mum was when she had been dead for years would have been a bit of a disaster. It turns out that Violet's mum, Sarah, was alive and well and living above the grocer's shop in the high street with her mum and dad, who were also alive and well. I hadn't managed to find out yet if I had any other family but I felt sure that would come over the next few days. I knew I had a mother as Violet had mentioned that in one of her letters.

Finally Violet said that she had to be up at five o clock the following morning and that she needed to go to bed. If I'm honest, I had been desperate to hear those words ever since we had that first kiss in the front parlour. We carefully put out all the gas lights and wound the mantle clocks in the living room and the parlour, which I felt was very quaint, but I suppose very necessary - if you needed to know the time. Violet led me up the stairs. We checked on the girls in their room and they were sleeping soundly. We then went through into the front bedroom, our bedroom. It was sparsely furnished with a large high double bed in the centre of one wall and a large mahogany double wardrobe along the adjoining wall. Next to that was a matching small mahogany dressing table. I noticed straight away that there was no en-suite. In fact there was no bathroom or toilet upstairs at all. I wasn't sure how that was going to work, where was I going to pee during the night? I was getting a bit worried about the two pints of beer I had just drunk. Where were we going to shower? I'd just have to face that one in the morning I thought. Luckily I had a good soak in a hot bath just before I had left Merryflats Hospital in Govan. Was that yesterday or the day before? Everything seemed such a blur. So all in all my level of hygiene wasn't too bad, all things considered. The scarring on my leg was pretty horrendous though and I was worried about undressing in front of Violet and letting her see it - never mind the fact that to me we were still complete strangers. Violet undressed in the corner of the room by the wardrobe and quickly slipped a long cotton night gown over her head before taking off her underwear. I tried not to stare at her while she did it. I took my clothes off quickly and it felt so good to get out of that uniform at last. I threw it over a chair in the corner and then limped over to the bed, pulling back the eiderdown and blankets and then sliding myself in under the cold sheets. It was a bit of an effort with my lame leg but I thankfully managed it with some decorum. Violet looked at me strangely.

'What's wrong?' I asked.

'Why didn't you put your pyjamas on?'

'I didn't know I had any,' I responded.

'Silly, of course you do. They're all neatly folded in the wardrobe, where they always used to be,' Violet said.

'Ah well, we probably won't be needing them anyway will we?' I said with my best puppy dog eyes. I could have sworn that Violet's face went a deep crimson, although it could have just been a trick of the gas light. Violet turned down the light and slid in her side of the bed.

'Why are you on the wrong side?' she asked once she was under the covers.

'Er I don't know,' I stammered again. 'I think it was just easier to get in this side with my leg,' I suggested.

'You poor thing, then that will be your side from now on,' she said as she slid closer to me. I put my arms around her and we cuddled in close to each other under the cold sheets.

'Does your leg hurt really badly?' Violet asked in a very concerned voice.

'No my love it's fine.' It could have been a lot worse I thought, remembering those terrible gas cases I had seen. I shuddered; I didn't want to think about it. Not now.

'Are you cold my love?' said Violet, drawing me in closer.

'A little,' I said as my lips found her soft sweet tasting ones. We lay there just holding and kissing each other, both enjoying the moment, not wanting it to end.

'I never thought we would be together again George, I thought I had lost you,' Violet whispered, starting to cry again.

'Shh my love,' I said placing my finger against her lips. 'We're together again now.'

With that I scooped her small body up with my arm and rolled her onto me in one swift movement. As she sat astride me with an amazed look on her face I slipped her nightdress over her head, tossing it onto the floor, and eased myself into her, slowly. Violet leaned down and kissed me deeply as we began to move together. It was heavenly bliss. I had never in all my life experienced anything like it, my emotions were now completely out of control. The love I felt for Violet at that moment came from somewhere deep within and flooded across my entire body. I felt tears welling up and streaming freely down my face, and when I looked up I noticed tears were running down Violet's cheeks too as we made love in the romantic half-light of the flickering gas lamps. I had never cried while making love before, it just seemed so right and not silly at all. We made love twice that night before we finally fell asleep in each other's arms.

I don't remember dreaming anything during the night, thankfully. I just remember having a lovely warm cosy feeling inside whenever I stirred. The bed was very comfy even though I did get a bit tangled up in the sheets. I couldn't remember when duvets were invented; I hoped it would be soon, sheets were a nightmare. Waking up next to the beautiful smiling and very naked Violet was one of the other best moments of my life. If this was all a dream, I hoped with my all my heart that it was never going to end. The small alarm clock on the bedside table next to me started to ring loudly. I fumbled with it for a few moments until Violet reached over and took it from me, turning off the alarm. It was five AM.

'Uuugh,' I groaned. This was far too early. I usually set my digital alarm to wake me up at eight o clock so that I could be at the shop by nine o clock.

'Why do we have to get up so early?' I moaned as I reached out to Violet for another cuddle.

'Well Sarah will be here at seven o clock to look after the girls and I have to make up the fire, get some hot water going, get washed, dressed and get the breakfast ready before that, and then I have to get to work by seven thirty.'

I smiled sweetly at her as I rolled her back on top of me again. I was going to try and roll on top of Violet but I wasn't sure what would actually happen to my leg and I really didn't want to ruin the moment.

'So that's your little game is it?' smiled Violet coyly as she started to enjoy herself.

'You're going to make me late for work, old Mr Kempster won't be very pleased,' she protested, laughing.

We lay there for a few moments afterwards catching our breath before Violet finally got up and turned up the gas lamp. She slipped on her nightgown and pulled on a thick woollen dressing gown over the top before disappearing downstairs to start her chores. I lay there thinking. Usually I would lay back now and turn on the TV in my bedroom and start to catch up on what was going on in the world before I went off to work. I was starting to realise that was the strange thing with this world in 1918, you were completely cut off inside your home. There was no television, no radio and no phone. Nothing. No idea as to what was happening outside. We were at the end of perhaps the greatest war in history, a world war, and I had no idea what was going on. I guessed everyone here must just rely on newspapers as the only source of news? And of course local gossip I guess. How did everyone survive?

I sat up and carefully slid my legs over the side and onto the floor whilst grabbing my walking stick which was still leaning against the bedside table. With a sort of twisting motion I managed to stand upright without too much fuss or pain. I limped over on the cold linoleum floor to the wardrobe and peered inside. I found a man's blue and red dressing gown hanging up on the left hand side so I grabbed that and pulled it on. It fitted me perfectly. It was certainly very chilly in the house so I needed something warm. I then surveyed the other clothes in the wardrobe. Violet had a few dresses hanging up on the right hand side and there were three pairs of tired looking shoes sitting underneath. She didn't seem to have much. On my side there was a dark blue suit hanging up and a number of pairs of brown trousers and greyish white shirts, all without collars. No denims, tee shirts or sweat shirts. Underneath I saw two pairs of brown leather boots. One pair was reasonably new and highly polished and the other had obviously seen much better days. On the top shelf were some long underpants, a few string vests, a load of what looked like collars for the shirts and some caps, three brown ones and two black. They looked like those funny flat caps you see the working men wearing in all the old newsreel films from the early part of the twentieth century. All in all it wasn't much of a choice I thought, and where were the trainers? This was all going to take a bit of getting used to.

I walked carefully down the stairs to see what Violet was up to. I found her in the living room on her knees in front of the fireplace.

'Just getting this lit my darling, I've made us some tea and it's on the table over there, still in the pot.'

I went over to the table and poured the tea into two cups through the strainer. I had seen it done in old films on the TV so I knew what to do. It made me smile.

'You sit there and drink your tea. The paper will be here soon as long as little Jimmy hasn't slept in again. I used to spend ten minutes every morning looking for any news from the front that mentioned your regiment. It never did, but I read it anyway. I won't be bothering this morning, it's all yours,' she said cheerfully.

'I've left some hot water in the basin in the kitchen for you to wash,' Violet said as she took her tea and went upstairs to see to the girls.

I drank my tea and then went into the kitchen where I found a large tin basin full of piping hot water with a strange smelling square bar of green soap and a towel next to it. I took my dressing gown off and washed myself as best as I could, standing there shivering on the freezing cold flagstone tiled floor. This was definitely going to take some getting used to. Not knowing whether I should tip the water away or not, I left it there, pulled on my dressing gown again and went back upstairs. The girls were dressed and sitting on our bed, which had already been made. Violet certainly had her act together in this house; I was totally impressed. Violet was just pulling on a very baggy shirt over a pair of old brown trousers. It looked like it might have been one of my shirts and it swamped her, but she still managed to look stunning and very sexy in it.

'Why are you wearing that?' I asked.

'What? Don't you find me attractive in my work clothes?' Violet laughed.

If only she knew.

I wondered what work Violet actually did and had to ask her.

'Darling, I'm doing your job for old Mr Kempster, I have been thcsc past three years, I told you in my letters. Women are out there working now you know, we are as good as you,' she said with a more serious look than I had yet seen on her face.

'I bloody know you are babe,' I laughed. 'Better! You all are.'

'George Puttnam! I've told you about your swearing and that's enough, especially in front of the girls. And why are you calling me a babe?'

I laughed again, and walked over to her, taking her in my arms. She couldn't stay mad at me for long.

'What should I wear today?' I asked, seriously not knowing what to put on and wanting to change the subject.

'Why don't you put on your Sunday suit darling?' Violet suggested.'You can come with me to see Mr Kempster to find out if you can get your old job back and I'm sure everyone else will want to see you too, so you'll have to look your best. Then you'll have to go and see your mum and dad and the rest of the family over on the high street. They won't even know you are home yet.'

That shook me, on two counts. I hadn't thought about what I was going to do for work - TVs and radios hadn't been invented yet, and I definitely hadn't thought about my mum or dad? I've never known a mum or dad.

Violet took the girls downstairs for their breakfast while I struggled into my suit. It was very slightly on the big side for me but it wasn't too bad a fit. Maybe I had lost weight at the front? The braces were a bit of a novelty but I soon managed to work out how they buttoned onto my trousers. I also managed to get my sock on eventually, for the first time unaided, but I had no luck with my boot, I'd have to get Violet to do that. I looked in the mirror. Hmmm not bad I thought. Reasonably presentable for a war hero. I smiled at that. I still couldn't think of myself as a war hero. If I'm honest I felt a bit of a fraud, but still, in everyone's eyes here I had been in the front line since August 1915, that's three and a half years in the trenches, and I had made it home alive. That was surely something to celebrate. I picked up my boots and walked downstairs.

'Well don't you just look like my handsome hero?' said Violet as I walked into the living room. She came over and put her arms around me. 'But where's your cap?' she asked, looking up at my head.

'I'm not wearing one of those. I'd look ridiculous,' I said.

Violet looked strangely at me but obviously decided to let it pass.

'There's some bread and jam on the table and more tea in the pot,' she said as she disappeared back into the kitchen. I'll be back in a minute to help you with your boots,' she said over her shoulder as she walked away. I poured myself another cup of tea and wandered through into the front parlour. It was cold in there but I liked the room. It was peaceful. I made a mental note to make sure we used it more often. I stood in the bay window drinking my tea while I glanced up and down the road in the early morning light. There were a few people walking up and down but it was so strange to see no cars parked in the street. There wouldn't be many for another 30 years or so I figured. It was then that I noticed the tall gangly figure in the long dark coat standing across on the other side of the street. He was staring straight at me. Although no longer in uniform his features were unmistakable; it was the soldier from back in my flat in 1984 again. I stood there transfixed for a second or two, my tea cup poised half way to my mouth. Then I reacted, throwing the cup down onto the table next to me I ran, well limped quickly, to the door and out into the hallway. Reaching the front door I slammed back the bolt, turned the big key, pulled open the door and ran out into the street. The man was gone. I looked up and down the street but he was nowhere to be seen. I limped across the road leaning heavily on my stick, still in my socks, and looked over the low wall behind where he had been standing. Nothing, he had completely vanished. I turned around and Violet was standing there at our front gate, with Evelyn and Daisy behind her.

'What's wrong George? What are you doing?' she asked.

'Oh, nothing my love. I thought I just saw someone I knew and I tried to catch him. But he's gone.'

'Please come in George, you don't even have your boots on.'

I followed the girls back into the house, my mind in turmoil.

As we went back inside, Violet's mum, Sarah, turned up. Sarah was certainly a young mother, just over forty years old and I could see immediately where Violet got her looks from; a striking and very attractive woman. As soon as she saw me she flung her arms around me and kissed me. I loved this already.

'George, you're alive! When did you get home? You're looking great but how is the leg?'

'Yes I certainly hope I am alive. I'm well thank you Sarah and I'm managing to cope with the leg, it's not too bad now.'

'Tell me about the front George, what was it like?' Sarah asked.

'Now Mum, not now, we don't have time. You can quiz George later on,' said Violet as she and Sarah gathered the girls up and took them into the living room. Violet and I said our goodbyes and disappeared out of the front door. As we walked up the hill to the smithy at Boat Inn Yard, just at the top of George Street, my mind was again on the sinister tall soldier.

'A penny for your thoughts George?' said Violet.

'Ah sorry my love, I'm just a bit distracted,' I said, grabbing her hand and squeezing it tightly.

'Was it that man you just saw, is there a problem?' asked Violet, perceptibly.

'Er no my love, I'll tell you about it later. Is that old Mr Kempster there standing outside the smithy?' I asked, grateful for a reason to change the subject. The man standing outside the smithy was leaning over with both hands on a stout wooden walking cane. He was dressed in brown leather working boots, baggy brown trousers, an old brown suit jacket and a striped collarless shirt with braces just visible underneath. He had a shock of unkempt white hair on the top of his head which was poking out under a flat brown cap. A thick bushy white beard covered the lower part of his face. Although looking haggard and slightly stooped, it was easy to see that he had been a powerfully built man in his prime.

'Yes it is darling. Let's go and meet him,' said Violet.

'George! I had no idea you were home. It's so good to see you back and doing well ... well apart from the stick of course. Was it a bad wound?' asked Mr Kempster with a genuine look of concern in his eyes as he shook my hand up and down.

'It was a gunshot wound which shattered my right knee Mr Kempster. It was painful but I'm managing well enough now thank you.'

'Come on in son, come on in. Let's get the kettle on and you can tell me all about it,' said Mr Kempster as he led us in through the open double doors of the smithy. It was quite dim inside compared to the strong sunlight we had just stepped out of, and it was stifling hot. Looking quickly around I spotted that there were two furnaces already roaring in the workshop and the heat coming off them was almost unbearable. There were some large pieces of equipment positioned around the place that I had absolutely no idea what they could be used for. I also noticed two old fashioned looking bicycles leaning against a bench and another one positioned upside down in a frame, obviously in the process of being worked on. It was a completely alien environment for me.

'I'll get on with my work while you two talk,' said Violet as she walked over to a bench, picking up a large pair of leather gloves.

I gave her an admiring glance over my shoulder as Mr Kempster and I walked through a door in the back of the workshop which led into a very small back office. There was a wooden desk in the centre of the tiny room, a large wooden swivel chair sat behind that and a tired old looking wooden filing cabinet was sitting in one corner of the room. The desk was covered in paperwork and the in-tray was virtually overflowing onto the floor. There were papers stacked up on top of the filing cabinet and also scattered around in small piles all over the floor. It was a bit of a mess to say the least.

'Please sit here George,' said Mr Kempster, indicating the large chair behind the desk. 'I'll get the tea on,' he said as he disappeared through another door at the rear of the office. I sat in the chair and looked at the chaos in front of me. There were invoices laying there and monthly account statements all mixed up with receipts from suppliers and letters from customers. There seemed to be little or no system at all for dealing with administration here. I had no idea how he managed to run the business at all like this.

Mr Kempster was soon back carrying two mugs of steaming tea. Swiping aside some paperwork he set them down on the desk before dragging over a wooden stool that he perched himself on.

'George, it is really good to see you again, safe and sound. How was it at the front? We're hearing some real horror stories from one or two of the lads who have come back wounded but the papers are not saying too much on that. The continuing daily lists of dead in the papers tell their own story though. How bad was it George?'

'Pretty bad Mr Kempster, but the lads are holding up and it will all be over very soon.' I tried to put as positive a spin on it as I could.

'Is that right George? Why do you think that? The papers are saying that this war could go on for years yet?'

'Believe me Mr Kempster; it will be over in weeks. The Germans are struggling and their economy is collapsing at home. Their soldiers at the front are getting no food or supplies and I believe that things have already begun to collapse there and they will have to give up soon. Anyway, how are things going here with you?' I said, feeling uncomfortable and trying to change the subject.

Mr Kempster then went on to tell me how he didn't mind admitting that he was struggling. Backing up what Violet had already told me, he said that he had no other family apart from his ailing wife at home, and there were no other young men in the village that could have helped out after I had left to go to the front. He said he was extremely grateful for all the help Violet had given and that she had kept the business running almost single-handed. He reckoned he would have had to have closed it long ago without her help. But he was still concerned that he was running into trouble. Violet couldn't do all of the physical work and all of the administration as well and Mr Kempster admitted that he was unable to do any physical work any longer and that his own eyesight had deteriorated so much over the past couple of years that he couldn't see to do the paperwork either. Things were getting into a real mess, as was evident from the paperwork in the office.

Although my army papers stated that I was an experienced 'shoeing smith' by trade, I had no real idea what that entailed. As I had walked through the workshop earlier I could see that the activities obviously involved a lot of metal-work and the repairing of various household items, tools and bicycles as well as the re-shoeing of horses, and judging by the number of harnesses and saddles hanging up around the place there was also a certain amount of tannery work involved too. It would be a steep learning curve for me but I reasoned that with Violet's help I would be able to get things back on track for Mr Kempster, even though I wasn't sure yet how I would explain why I couldn't remember how to do anything.

'Mr Kempster, I'm back now and if you'll take me back on, as a partner, Violet and I can get things sorted here. We can run the business between us, including the paperwork and you can go home and look after your wife. I can come by every Friday evening and give you an update on how things are running. You can trust us Mr Kempster, we will look after the business and you can relax. If you agree I will start work here again tomorrow,' I said earnestly.

Mr Kempster beamed at me across the desk. 'Thank you George, thank you. That's exactly what I have been wanting to hear. You are a real life saver, a real life saver. How can I ever repay you?'

'You already have Mr Kempster, you already have. You have looked after Violet and my girls while I was away at the front and now you have given me another chance. Thank you Mr Kempster,' I said as we shook hands on the deal over the desk.

I left a happy and smiling Mr Kempster standing in front of the smithy with his arm around Violet's shoulder. Violet gave me a little wave as I limped off down the hill towards the high street and my parent's smithy. I hoped I would be able to find it.

I walked down Ravens Lane towards the high street with my stomach in knots, yet again. I couldn't ask Violet where my parents' smithy business actually was, she would have thought I'd gone mad so I just hoped the village would be small enough that I'd find it easily. I didn't know how I was going to react when I met my parents for the first time. Violet had said that I had brothers and sisters but I couldn't ask too much about them so I had no real idea who they all were. If I got into trouble I figured I would just have to rely on the old backup story and say I had a bit of amnesia from concussion at the front. I felt sure everyone would understand. As I reached the high street I realised it wouldn't be too difficult to find them. The village was very small and very empty, nothing at all like the bustling Berkhampsted town I remembered from 1984. The high street was very quiet with just the odd motorised vehicle driving noisily past and a number of horse and carts moving up and down the cobbled road. There were people milling about though so I asked an elderly lady walking by where I might find the smithy on the high street - I assumed there would be only one. She pointed up the road on the other side.

'It's about a three minute walk for you young man, and about a fifteen minute one for me,' she said smiling.

I crossed over and walked along the high street until I came to a large painted metal sign announcing '*Puttnam's Shoeing and General Smith*' hanging up over a big old white painted building, just on the edge of the village. It was obviously very much bigger than Mr Kempster's workshop. There were various bikes, garden tools, carts, wheels and even an old mangle all dumped haphazardly in the front yard area outside the workshop. I approached the large open double wooden doors and peered inside. There appeared to be quite a bit of activity going on with at least four people working hard at the furnaces and the numerous work benches inside the building. The heat and the noise were almost unbearable. I had no idea at all how anyone could work inside in these conditions.

'George!' someone shouted from behind. I turned around and there stood my Father. I knew he was my father the moment I set eyes on him; it was like looking in a mirror at an older version of me.

'Son!' was all he said as he came over and hugged me tightly. I could have cried.

'When did you get home? How are you? Let me look at you,' he said as he stepped back to look at me. I could see dampness in his eyes.

'I got home late last night, and yes I'm fine. Bit of a wound in my right knee but otherwise all OK. How is everyone?' I asked, hoping I'd gather some more info.

'Everyone's grand George,' Dad said, beaming from ear to ear. 'Albert and Young William are still at the front but I think all is OK with them, no news being good news eh? Everyone else here is just grand and they'll all be very happy to see you George. Let's go on up and see Mother.'

Dad put his arm around my shoulders and guided me around the side of the workshop and up a metal staircase at the rear of the building. Reaching the top, he pushed open a large black painted door and we walked in and down a long thin hallway.

'Mother, Mother, where are you?' Dad shouted.

'In the kitchen dear,' came the reply from the end of the hallway.

Dad walked with his massive arm around my shoulder towards the kitchen door and pushed me in ahead of him. In front of the kitchen range stood a smiling, slightly plump, red faced, middle-aged lady with neat pinned back dark brown hair, wearing a floral pinafore dress.

'George!' she screamed as she rushed over to me and hugged me close, almost knocking me over.

'How are you my boy?' she cried, tears of joy streaming down her rosy cheeks.

'I'm fine mum,' I said, with tears in my eyes too now.

'I'll put the kettle on,' she said. Why do mums always resort to putting the kettle on? Personally I thought I needed something a little stronger. Dad took a pipe out of his jacket pocket and started to light it from a piece of paper he had just lit at the kitchen range. Watching him puff furiously on his pipe I remembered that I hadn't had a cigarette since yesterday evening. Ah bugger! I had left my packet of Woodbines in my army tunic pocket in the wardrobe. Oh well, it's probably time to give it up anyway I thought.

Mum and Dad took it in turns to ask me all about my life at the front, my wound and how I had got home. I thankfully managed to dodge most of the difficult questions and did manage to glean some more information on my family. It seemed I had three brothers, with Albert and William at the front and young Lawrence who was still at school, and I had three sisters, two at school and one working up at the munitions factory over in Hemel Hempstead.

After about three cups of tea I agreed to allow Mum and Dad to organise a family get together for the following Sunday so that I could get to see everyone and they could get to welcome me home properly. I then made my excuses and left, allowing Dad to go back to work and Mum to start her preparations.

As I walked back up the high street I thought I'd go for a walk through the village first to see how things looked in 1918 and perhaps stop for a pie and a pint somewhere before I went back home. I had a few shillings in my pocket, I hoped that would be enough.

Chapter Eleven

Berkhampsted, Hertfordshire, England - 18 November 1918

The 11th November 1918 was an exceptional day by anyone's account. It was a Monday morning and Violet, the girls and I were all up early ready to start our week. We had just spent a wonderful peaceful day off on Sunday with the girls, having a picnic over in the castle grounds. How they enjoyed running around the castle ruins playing knights and...well…bad knights. I hadn't done that since I was a kid and I'd forgotten what simple fun it could be. Sunday was the one day we had off during the week so we had to make the most of it. I put my foot in it on the Sunday evening though after a few beers by telling Violet that the armistice was being signed the next day on the 11th at 11.00am. She asked me how I knew that and I think I mumbled something about reading it somewhere. It would probably come back to haunt me later on today when the news got around and Violet started quizzing me again.

I remembered from my history lessons and the project I had done for my O'Level exams that the actual armistice was agreed and signed at around 05.00am that Monday morning, but with hostilities not actually planned to cease until 11.00am to allow for the information to travel across the whole of the Western Front. The basic telegraph technology of this time enabled the news to reach each of the key capital cities by around 05.40am and therefore celebrations had already begun at home long before very many soldiers at the front even knew about the Armistice. In London, Big Ben was going to be rung for the first time since the start of the war in August 1914 and in Paris, gas lamps were going to be lit for the first time in four years. I also knew that tragically many tens of thousands of soldiers assumed that it was just another day in the war and many officers continued to order their men into combat. Quite a number of those final casualties were at Mons in Belgium which was ironically one of the first major battles of the war in August 1914. I remembered reading that in a cemetery just outside of Mons in the village of Nouvelle;

there are nine graves of British soldiers. Five are from August 1914 while four are dated November 11th 1918.

Horrifically the Americans took some really heavy casualties on this last day of the war because their commander, General John Pershing, believed that the Germans had to be severely defeated at a military level to effectively 'teach them a lesson'. Pershing saw the terms of the Armistice as being too soft on the Germans therefore he supported those commanders who wanted to be pro-active in attacking German positions, even though he knew that an Armistice had been signed. The 89th US Division was ordered to attack and take the town of Stenay on the morning of November 11th. Stenay was the last town captured on the Western Front but at a cost of 300 casualties. The Americans alone suffered over 3,000 casualties on that last morning.

I remember writing in my project that the last British soldier killed in World War One was a Private George Edwin Ellison of the 5th Royal Irish Lancers. He was killed at Mons - where he had also fought in 1914 - at 09.30am, just 90 minutes before the ceasefire. He had spent the whole four years of the war at the front and then died 90 minutes before the end. I remembered thinking how absolutely tragic that was.

I recall that the last French soldier to die was a runner and he was in the process of taking a message to his colleagues at the front informing them of the ceasefire. He was hit by a single shot and killed at 10.50am. In total, 75 French soldiers were killed on November 11th but their graves actually state November 10th. I learned that two theories were put forward for this discrepancy. The first was that by stating they had died on November 10th before the war had ended, there could be no question about their family's entitlement to a war pension. The other theory was that the French government wanted to avoid any form of embarrassment or political scandal should it ever become known that so many died on the last morning of the war.

The very last American soldier killed was Private Henry Gunter who was killed at 10.59am. I believe that officially, Gunter was the last man to die in World War One. His unit had been ordered to advance and take a German machine gun post. It is said that even the Germans – who knew that they were literally minutes away from a ceasefire – had tried to stop the Americans attacking, but when it became obvious that this had failed, they had to defend themselves so they fired on their attackers and Gunter was killed.

Officially over 10,000 men were killed, wounded or went missing on November 11th 1918. That was a tragic fact of that last day which was being celebrated by so many people across the world. It hit me hard to think that sadly, all of that was going on over in France and Belgium whilst I sat there that Monday morning eating my toast. What a waste of life.

I knew that today was going to be something else and I reckoned that the news would be reaching us 'formally' by the time we had got to the smithy that morning. I also guessed that we weren't likely to be getting much work done today, so out of respect for all the people still at the front I decided to put my uniform on for this special occasion. Also, for purely selfish reasons, I always thought it must have been great to be in uniform on the actual Armistice Day, and also VE Day at the end of World War 2 - what with all that kissing and hugging going on, so I just indulged myself. When I came down the stairs in my nicely cleaned and pressed uniform with my peaked cap tucked under my arm, Violet eyed me with a look of worry.

'What are you up to George, where are you going in that?'

'Nowhere my love, just to work with you. But as I said last night, I do think we are going to be getting some news today and I wanted to dress for the occasion.'

'Yes you mentioned that last night,' Violet said, and eyed me up and down suspiciously. 'But we've heard nothing about that George. I read all the papers yesterday and there was nothing in there about the war ending. I would like to think I would have remembered reading that? Where did you get the information George, we haven't even had the morning papers yet?'

We knew that the war must be drawing to a close soon. The papers were full of the fact that the Kaiser had abdicated and had fled to Holland and now there were riots in Berlin which were being reported over the weekend. It felt like it was all coming to a close, but people like Violet had lived with this nightmare for four long years now and although they wanted to believe it was almost over, most people would have had difficulty accepting it, at least until it was officially announced in the papers anyway.

'Oh look, here's Sarah,' I said, quickly trying to change the subject.

Mother-in-Law Sarah came in to mind the girls and immediately started to rib me about my uniform. She said I looked dashing and gave me a longer kiss than usual - which was a bit of an awkward moment.

Violet and I marched arm in arm up the road and had just opened the doors to the smithy at 07.30am on the dot when Jimmy the post boy came running down the street shouting 'the war's over, the war's over, it's really over. The armistice is being signed at 11.00am. It's over!' Front doors started to open and people began to gather in the street. Chatting, smiling, crying, and not daring to believe that it was perhaps finally really over.

Violet looked at me with her hands on her hips and a fake stern look on her face.

'How did you know George?'

'Mmm just call it premonition my love, I'll tell you about it later. For now, I'll go over to old Sidney at the Boat Inn and arrange for a couple of kegs of beer to be brought out so that we can buy everyone a drink. You get the other neighbours together and get some sandwiches organised. Call my Mum and Dad too? Let's have a party!'

'Call your Mum and Dad? What from here?' queried Violet.

'Mmm good point,' I mumbled.

Violet and I kissed and hugged and then she ran off with the biggest smile on her face. The party we had that day was absolutely superb. No one went to work and none of the children went to school. It wasn't expected as it seemed everyone all over the country had taken the day off. The neighbours up and down the street dragged out chairs and tables and a lot of cake baking and sandwich making went on all day. The kids played in the street and there was a whole lot of singing, eating, kissing and many many tears. No one had been unaffected by this war it seemed. We had to go and get one or two of our friends out who were home alone, widows now. Mind you, they took some coaxing, understandably, but most joined in to some degree eventually. Someone dragged an old piano out into the street and the beer and sherry flowed. It was a time for relief and letting off steam. Most of us were three parts to the wind by tea time. Mum, Dad and my sisters and young Lawrence came over in the late afternoon and the drinking started again in earnest.

Despite the frivolities, the cheering and the singing, the celebrations were tinged with an underlying sense of sadness for everybody. There wasn't a family in the street who hadn't lost someone or who still had a husband, father, brother or lover at the front. In my short time over there in France I had met many brave people, many who had helped me in my hour of need. I knew that those still out there on the front lines would not be celebrating. They would most likely have nothing to celebrate with and I imagine all they would be feeling would be a surreal silence and emptiness after 52 exhausting months of war. The nurses and the doctors would still be patching up the broken bodies and the soldiers would undoubtedly just be waiting for hostilities to begin again. They would not yet believe that the war was actually over and probably wouldn't for some time to come. The flu pandemic was raging across the world now as well, and millions were dying of that. The human race had a lot of mending to do and there was undoubtedly still a lot of pain to go through for many, and today was just day one of that healing process for most of us.

I went to bed very drunk that night. Violet put me to bed and tucked me in, pretending to scold me like a naughty child but kissing me on the forehead and smiling at the same time. The girls wanted to know what had happened to Daddy and I heard Violet whispering to them that I had eaten too much cake as she quietly closed the bedroom door. Yes, too much cake I thought, smiling.

Chapter Twelve

Berkhampsted, Hertfordshire, England - 11 July 1919

The months seemed to be flashing by in a blur in this, my new life. Everything was so new and exciting and I was still coming to terms with having someone love me as much as Violet and the girls so obviously did. I had no difficulty in loving them right back, just as deeply. It has been all I have ever dreamed of, and now I had it all. A loving family and a wonderful future ahead of us. I had all but forgotten my past life back - or forward depending on how you looked at it - in 1984. I had managed to relegate that past existence now to just a nagging troublesome feeling which sat at the back of my mind and only came to the surface occasionally, usually in those sleepless moments in the dark of the night. Thinking of my old life now gave me a cold feeling, a sense of unease and a worrying thought that someday, somehow, this wonderful life might all be taken away from me and I might find myself back in my lonely flat in 1984 again.

Violet managed to teach me a bit in the workshop and I was now a dab hand at mending bikes and could just about manage to produce a reasonable horse shoe. Violet just couldn't get her head around why I seemed not to be able to remember how to do the work in the smithy as apparently I was one of the best shoeing smiths in the county before I had joined up. I think I had managed to convince her that I must have taken some concussion when I was wounded in France and that was why I appeared to have forgotten everything; a touch of amnesia. Violet took me to the doctor about it but he quickly dismissed it and put it down to the stress of the war. I suspected he didn't know quite what to do about it anyway and he probably had far worse cases he was having to deal with every day. I suspect many ailments got put down to the stress of war in those days.

In addition to the amnesia Violet also said I had changed in other ways. In the beginning I was constantly getting funny looks from her with the strange way I talked and the phrases I used.

Fortunately that had at least got a bit better recently as I adapted to the language and culture of this early part of the 20th century. She said that my new open and very public affection for her and the girls since coming back from the war was a definite improvement and she certainly didn't want to change that, but she still thought that something was very different about me and couldn't quite put her finger on it. If only she knew.

The smithy business was doing really well. At the start Violet and I shared the administration and the physical work and we worked very well together, but I was now doing pretty much all of the physical work as her nearly nine month bump was beginning to get in the way. I was getting somewhat paranoid and kept telling her to stay in the office, sitting down, but she insisted that pregnancy wasn't an illness and she reminded me how she had beaten out carpets and scrubbed floors and generally looked after the house - and me - whilst she had carried Daisy. Eventually I won the argument and we took on a young local lad James. He had sadly lost a good part of his face on the Somme in 1916 but he still had one good eye and was very conscientious. His fixed plastic smile drew a lot of sympathetic looks and a few scared ones from the children, but on the whole most local people had managed to get over his disfigurement and just saw him for the hard working gentle lad he was. He always reminded me of the young lad I saw in the trench that day with half of his face scythed off by a shell. I always wondered what had happened to him and whether he made it. With James's help, everything was tidy and running smoothly now. Dad was sending over many of the smaller jobs he couldn't take on and our order books were full for three months in advance. With James around I did manage to find some time to start dabbling in building crystal radio sets. Radio was highly specialist and hadn't really taken off as yet, but I wasn't going to let that stop me. I had decided that with my knowledge of radio I could get way ahead of the game. I didn't plan on mending bicycles and fitting shoes on horses for the rest of my life.

I already knew of course that radio broadcasting in Britain began in 1920 with Marconi's experimental station 2MT which was located in an ex-army hut down in Writtle, Essex. The station was initially allowed to transmit its test transmissions for only half an hour a week but I remembered from my time at Salford University that Dame Nellie Melba was famously to make one of the first broadcasts from Writtle at 7.10 pm on the 15th June 1920. This consisted of a concert of opera music to entertain the listeners, and it was only a year away from now. From what I could remember reading at Uni, the broadcast opened with a recital of Home Sweet Home and finished - unsurprisingly - with the national anthem. It was big news in the radio world and I knew that the early radio amateurs would soon be tuning into the broadcasts from London to Paris and even Berlin. It was a very exciting time in the development of radio and not only was I here at this particular time, I knew what was going to happen and when. And perhaps more importantly for me, at this moment in time I probably understood more about the science of radio than any other person on the planet - unless there were other time travellers around of course.

By February 1922, the army hut in Writtle would commence broadcasting daily half hour programmes of news and entertainment. Listeners would tune in using crystal sets, the simplest form of radio receiver that needed no external power or batteries. All that powers the headphones of a basic crystal set is the energy collected from its aerial which is derived from the radio waves sent by the transmitter of the radio station to which the set is tuned. This was just as well as no one around here seemed to have electricity in their homes as yet. I was in the fortunate position that I could make these crystal sets with my eyes closed. In fact, I made my first basic crystal radio when I was only about seven years old using a very basic radio kit which I had been given by someone in the care home one Christmas. That present had almost certainly been responsible for my enduring obsession with all things radio ever since. I was very wary of getting ahead of my time though, as I thought that here in 1919 it might be highly suspicious, but I was starting to plan ways of introducing massive improvements to the first basic transistors that were starting to be developed. I just couldn't help myself. Violet thought I was absolutely stark raving mad of course. She said it was all newfangled and would never catch on. It was just a toy for nut cases like me and would never have any real use. But I knew that by May 1922 Marconi's company would be in talks with wireless set manufactures and other interested organisations to set up more broadcasting stations around the country under an umbrella organisation which they planned on calling the British Broadcasting Company. The BBC. And I had every intention of being in on that one right at the start.

The only tragic event for us in the past nine months since my return was the very sad death of my younger brother Lawrence, back in April. The doctor believes it was TB mixed with the flu which killed him. He was only 17. Of course I didn't know him when I first came back and I hadn't really had a chance to get to know him that well since and that bothered me a lot. Life was so cruel and I knew that in another ten years or so the medical advancements would have saved him. It was a very sad time for all of us. Everyone missed young Lawrence. He would not be forgotten.

It was one very warm Friday morning in July when I heard Violet calling me from the workshop.

'George, there's someone here to see you.' Violet popped her head around the door of the office 'and he's a strange one at that,' she said, raising her eyebrows.

My heart stopped beating for a few seconds and my stomach lurched. I suddenly went very cold. It couldn't be the sinister soldier could it? Please not now? I didn't want to leave this life, I was just starting to relax. I absolutely adored Violet and the girls - and the bump - and I had our whole life mapped out. I just couldn't face going back to my old sad life now. I felt sick as I stood up and with my heart in my mouth I walked through to the workshop.

Standing there in front of the new wooden counter dressed in a new baggy brown suit was the imposing muscular figure of Karl. Karl the German. I let out the breath I wasn't aware I had been holding and smiled with relief.

'Karl, Karl, it's great to see you,' I said, pumping his hand up and down. Karl beamed back at me.

'It's great to see you again George, it truly is.'

'Violet come here and meet Karl, my old friend.'

Violet looked at me dumfounded.

'Is he German?' she asked in a whisper, but still loud enough for Karl to hear.

'Yes he is, and he saved my life so he is more than welcome here,' I whispered back, slightly louder.

'Pleased to meet you, er…Karl,' Violet said hesitatingly. She didn't make any move to shake his hand.

I understood, as I guessed Karl did also. We had been enemies for four long years in one of the most vicious wars that had ever been fought and many of Violet's friends and family had died at the hands of our enemy, the Germans. That wasn't going to be so easily forgotten. I came from a time when those differences had been patched up and we were all on the same side by then, I didn't perhaps see things the same way as people back here in 1919 did.

'How did you get here Karl? What are you up to?' I asked.

'Well it's a long story George. I was held in a prisoner of war camp over in the beautiful county of Wiltshire. I've been there since I was brought over here, just after we last saw each other back in March of last year. The camp was well run and our guards were very fair. We were put out to work most days in a nearby airfield at Yatesbury. That was good, it was very nice to get out and do some useful work instead of just being locked up behind barbed wire fences all the time. At Yatesbury they were training your pilots in air reconnaissance and we were there carrying out repairs to the runways and the tarmac. One day about a month ago there was a big crash. One of the trainee pilots crashed his Bristol fighter aircraft nose first into the end of the runway. The plane was on fire and the pilot couldn't get out. I was standing about 200 metres away with a group of prisoners when it came down so

I ran over to the burning wreckage and managed to pull the pilot out before the fuel ignited and the wreckage exploded. Because I had saved the young pilot's life, I was released forthwith, and given free rail and sailing tickets home to Germany. They also gave me this nice suit and some money, and a silver watch,' Karl said, proudly holding up a brand new silver pocket watch on a chain.

'Wow! Karl, that's some story,' I said, patting him on the back. Even Violet smiled, clearly impressed and looking a little more relaxed now.

'Come through and have a tea Karl, we have a lot to talk about,' I insisted.

I led Karl through to the back office and Violet went through to put the kettle on.

'So, you really are a hero then?' I ribbed him. 'Are you on your way home? How did you find me?'

Karl laughed to hide his embarrassment. 'Yes I guess I'm going home but I'm not sure what I will find there. I'm in no rush though and I wanted to find you again before I went back. I remembered that you said you lived in Berkhampsted and it wasn't too far from Wiltshire anyway so I just came here and started asking around. I was a bit worried, being a German wandering around in England. After the last four years of war I thought that many people understandably might not be too friendly towards me, but my English is pretty good and I have lived here before so I took a chance. I soon found out where you were, everyone around here seems to know you.' Karl smiled.

'It's great to see you again Karl. How long have you got?'

'Would it be all right if I stay around for a couple of days George? I would like to see more of this place.'

'Yes of course Karl and you must stay with us. We have a small spare bedroom, you won't be in the way and it will be safer anyway,' I said, looking at Violet for approval. She nodded discreetly and smiled at me, but I could tell she wasn't altogether too comfortable. The British propaganda about German soldiers had worked its stuff and virtually everyone believed that all German soldiers were murdering psychopaths, so it was to be expected.

'We'll have to call you Clive though, not Karl, if that's OK with you while you're here with us?'

'Yes that's perfect George, Violet, I like Clive, thank you.' Karl beamed again gratefully, looking at both of us.

Chapter Thirteen

Ducks Cross Camp, Colmworth, England - 1 June 1920

Hauptmann Von Schultz knocked loudly on Lieutenant Croft's office door.

'Come in,' shouted Lieutenant Croft. 'Ah, good evening Hauptmann, please come in and take a seat. What was it you wanted to see me about?'

Von Schultz walked into the office and sat down in the small chair opposite the Lieutenant's desk, placing a large book he had been carrying onto the desk in front of him.

'Lieutenant, as you know I have been working in the prison library for nearly two years now. I just wanted to say a big thank you for giving me the opportunity to undertake this work, and for allowing me to further develop the library, obtaining many new titles for the men. The work has been extremely rewarding and it has also allowed me personally to gain a much better understanding and working knowledge of your language, English, and I am very grateful for that. So I just wanted to come and say a really big thank you Lieutenant Croft for trusting me. Also, I know you are a very busy man but there is one thing I would very much appreciate it if you could help me with? I am having trouble understanding something,' said Von Schultz as he opened the book up to a bookmarked page.

'Of course Hauptmann, it would be a pleasure,' smiled Lieutenant Croft as he stood up and walked around the desk to look down at the book. As the Lieutenant bent down to look at the page of text, Von Schultz quickly wrapped his arms tightly around the Lieutenant's head and twisted it violently around until there was a loud crack and Lieutenant Croft's body went limp. There was no other sound; Lieutenant Croft never even had a chance to utter a cry. Von Schultz let the body slump to the floor and quickly stepped over to the door and turned the key in the lock. Moving back to the body, Von Schultz put his fingers to

Lieutenant Croft's twisted neck to make sure he was dead, although the blank staring eyes already suggested he very much was. Confirming that there was no longer a pulse, he began to remove the Lieutenant's uniform. It took about ten minutes to finally remove the Sam Browne belt and holster, the tunic, trousers and the long brown boots and quickly dress himself in the officer's uniform. Luckily the Lieutenant was roughly the same size as Von Schultz, which was why he had planned it this way. Von Schultz was significantly more muscular than the Lieutenant so the tunic was a bit of a snug fit, but it wasn't too bad. It would do for now.

Von Schultz dragged the body around to the back of the desk and did his best to hide it. He reasoned that it might buy him a few moments if someone only had a quick glance in the office. He took the Webley service revolver from the holster, checked that there were six rounds in the chambers and then put it back in the holster leaving the holster flap unfastened, just in case he needed to get to it quickly. He hoped not. He lifted the Lieutenant's bunch of keys from the desk, straightened his jacket, took a deep breath and unlocked the door. Confidence was the key here, Von Schultz knew that. He needed to walk quickly from the office to the Lieutenant's car parked out front, get in it and calmly drive to the exit gate. He hoped that the guard would simply lift the gate when he saw the Lieutenant's car, without looking too closely inside. However, if the guard did decide to get curious, Von Schultz was very prepared to shoot his way out.

Von Schultz made it out of the office and across to the car without bumping into anyone. The driver's door was unlocked, fortunately, so Von Schultz quickly slid into the worn leather seat and slammed the door shut. He took his pistol out and laid it in his lap, ready. Looking up, Von Schultz's heart sank when he saw Kapitan Gröner walking across the compound, towards the office. He was going to pass right in front of the car.

'Damn! That's all I need,' muttered Von Schultz.

The first two keys that he tried in the ignition wouldn't fit. Three more to go.

'What are all these damn keys for?' muttered Von Schultz again as the Kapitan came closer.

He would be upon him in about ten more seconds. Von Schultz had no problem with gunning the Kapitan down in cold blood, in fact he thought he would probably quite enjoy it, but he couldn't afford that to happen right now. He had a job to do and that was more important than his own pleasure. The guards would be upon him as soon as the first shots were fired and even though they all seemed quite inept, one of them would inevitably hit him in a firefight, and he only had six bullets. Hauptmann Von Schultz was many things, but stupid wasn't one of them.

The Kapitan was just drawing level with the front of the car when the next key slid into the slot and Von Schultz switched the ignition on. Still holding his breath, he pushed hard on the start button to the left of the steering wheel. Thankfully the engine fired first time and Von Schultz pushed down the clutch, slipped the car into gear and pulled away. The Kapitan stopped and looked at the car as it sped across the compound towards the gate. The Kapitan had an appointment to see the Lieutenant so he was surprised to see him leaving in his car, and in somewhat of a hurry too. He knew the guard would stop the car at the gate so the Kapitan started to walk quickly in that direction, hoping to still catch the Lieutenant at the gate. He reasoned that the Lieutenant had probably just forgotten about the meeting.

As Von Schultz drove up to the gate he could see the Kapitan in his rear view mirror, now following him to the gate.

'Interfering idiot,' he said, loudly to himself.

The guard was slow to leave his little hut so Von Schultz had to bring the car to a stop at the gate. The guard smiled and gave a friendly wave as he walked over to lift the gate. Von Schultz revved the engine and was ready to drop the clutch and get out of there as soon as the gate was up, but Kapitan Gröner's face appeared at his side window.

'Damn!' swore Von Schultz under his breath again.

Von Schultz turned and looked at the Kapitan. Kapitan Gröner's eyes widened in shock, not quite comprehending what he was seeing - Hauptmann Von Schultz dressed in a British officer's uniform, driving Lieutenant Croft's car. The Kapitan stepped backwards quickly as Von Schultz drew his revolver up, aimed and fired through the open window. The bullet smashed straight through the Kapitan's chest as he back peddled furiously. He was punched back violently for about six feet and then collapsed glassy eyed to the floor with blood spreading quickly across the front of his uniform. Von Schultz then turned and fired at the guard, hitting him twice, in the chest and stomach. The guard fell back into his hut while Von Schultz gunned the car through the now open gateway.

Once out onto the single track lane, Von Schultz careered dangerously through the countryside as fast as the small car could go. He figured that he had about an hour or so at best. The car had military markings on it so it was a dead giveaway and he knew he had to lose it soon, but he also wanted to put as much distance as he could between him and the camp before he did. He had been doing his research whilst he was working in the library and he knew where he was heading - the small village of Berkhampsted, in Hertfordshire was about fifty miles from his current location. Von Schultz had no idea where Unteroffizier Karl Von Ohain was, or even if he was still in England after all this time, but he knew where he was going to find George, and he planned to dispose of him quickly before he made his way back to Germany. Karl would just have to wait for now he thought.

Chapter Fourteen

Berkhampsted, Hertfordshire, England - 2 June 1920

Karl was working in the smithy that morning. He wasn't making horse shoes or mending bicycles or anything else as boring and mundane as that, he was building another new crystal radio set. Karl had been working closely with George over the past eleven months designing and building crystal radio sets. Before the war Karl had been studying at the University of Göttingen which specialised in fluid mechanics and aerodynamics. Karl's father was a professor of aerodynamics there and Karl had inherited his avid interest in all things that flew. In those first few days last year when Karl began staying with the Puttnams he had become extremely interested in the work George was doing in his workshop on radios and immediately saw the practical uses for this new science, especially in the field of communications with aircraft. Karl was extremely impressed with George's knowledge of radio science and his ideas on the potential applications for radio in the aviation industry, and he had asked George if he could stay on for a few more weeks to learn more. It was now nearly a year later and Karl was still learning. George and Karl had developed a mutual respect for each other's abilities and a definite bond had formed between them. After a month or two they had started to develop their new radio business in the workshop and they were now making and selling crystal radio sets to the growing band of radio enthusiasts across the country. Over the past few months they had already gained a reputation for making the highest quality and most efficient sets around. Their fame was spreading and radio buffs were coming from as far away as Birmingham and Bristol to purchase George and Karl's radio sets. The radio business had now far overtaken the smithy work in terms of revenue flowing into the business.

George had also made contact with Guglielmo Marconi and had already met him in London on two occasions over the past few months. Unsurprisingly, Marconi was astounded by George's knowledge of radio science and his ideas on how the current crystal sets could be greatly improved upon. He had even started to discuss transistorisation with him which impressed Marconi no end. Marconi was now trying to entice George to go and work with him down in his experimental radio establishment in Writtle, Essex, but George was holding back on this at the moment, mostly because he didn't want to be away from Violet and the children but also he was worried about working too close to someone like Marconi in case his suspicions were aroused about George's unexplainable knowledge of radio science.

George was out that fateful morning. He was visiting his father in his smithy on the high street and then he was going to the bank to deposit the week's takings. Karl didn't expect him back for at least another hour and a half. Violet was at home minding the girls and the new ten month old addition to the family, little Arthur, so Karl was looking after the shop. Fortunately Karl's accent was quite impeccable anyway and in the past year his English had become almost indistinguishable from that of the locals around them. He had been easily accepted as George's pal Clive from the West Country, and was well liked in the village. He was whistling while he worked with his huge frame huddled over the workbench.

There was a loud knock at the big wooden front doors.

'Come in, it's not locked,' shouted Karl without turning around.

The knock came again, only louder this time.

'I said please come in,' Karl shouted, louder this time.

When the third knock at the door came, Karl almost threw down the small screwdriver he had been using, muttered an obscenity under his breath and crossed the workshop floor to the large double doors.

'I said the door is open,' Karl grumbled as he pulled open the smaller left hand door. His eyes widened in horror when he saw the muzzle of a revolver pointing directly at his head.

'Whaaaa,' he stuttered.

'Move back inside Karl,' said Von Schultz, menacingly.

'I was just checking if you were alone, I presume by the fact that you took so long to answer you are here on your own?'

Karl didn't respond. His mind was still trying to comprehend why Hauptmann Von Schultz was here dressed in a British officer's uniform, and pointing a revolver at his head.

'I came here for George; you were the last person I expected to see Karl. You are making life very easy for me,' he said mockingly.

'What do you want Hauptmann? Why are you here? And why did you try to kill me in France, what have I done to you?' asked Karl.

'Ahh, that's too many questions Karl, and anyway it's a very long story. We don't have time for it all now. I just need to find George and then kill both of you and get on my way. Where is he?'

'He's not here.'

'I can see that. Where is he?'

'Out.'

'You're not being very co-operative are you Karl? I know where he lives anyway, the nice people in the post office told me. Number nine, just across the road.'

Karl didn't say anything, he just stood there grim faced, looking around and desperately trying to think of some way of turning this around and attacking Von Schultz.

'Karl, we're out of time. I have three rounds left in this revolver and I only want to use one on you, so stand still like a good boy and let me finish you off.'

Von Schultz smiled as he pulled back the hammer of the revolver just as Karl made his move forward. Karl had seen a large scythe hanging down from the ceiling, just in front of his head. He thought if he could just grab it and swing it in one motion he might be able to connect with Von Schultz's arm and knock the gun away from him before he fired it. Von Schultz was surprised by Karl's quick movement and stepped back quickly, firing at the same time. The sound of the .455 calibre round exploding from the gun was deafening in the close confines of the workshop. Karl stopped in midair and was thrown back against the wall with a large gaping wound in his chest. Sitting slumped against the wall, wheezing as the blood bubbled in gushes out of his destroyed lungs, Karl looked up at Von Schultz with an astonished look in his eyes.

'Sorry Karl. Truly I am. It's not personal; it's just something that has to be done. No hard feelings eh?' Von Schultz smiled down at Karl. He put the revolver back in his holster, turned on his heel and walked out of the workshop.

Karl's dying eyes stared blindly at the closing door.

Having done my duty and seen my parents for the first time this week I felt good. In fact life was pretty good all round, well apart from the outside loo of course and no bathroom at the house. I would definitely have to sort that soon. I had mentioned it to Violet several times that we needed an indoor toilet, bath and shower. She thought I'd gone mad again and suggested I must have picked up some strange ideas from my time in France. Violet said she always thought the French were an odd people, what with their funny toilet and washing ways. That always brought a smile to my face.

The takings from the smithy were doing well and the radio business was really booming. The money was rolling in and we were doing very well indeed. Even my leg wasn't giving me too much pain anymore. My two conversations with my all-time idol, the great Mr Guglielmo Marconi were probably two of the most fantastic moments of my life - well after meeting Violet, the girls and little Arthur of course. It was absolutely fascinating to hear his views and theories on radio waves and how he dreamed the current crystal sets might be utilised in the future. I had to keep pinching myself to remind me that I was actually talking to the great man. His dreams for the future were all in my past of course, which made it all the more fascinating. I knew what the future held and I was determined to be a big part of that future.

Karl had turned out to be a great help too. He has been helping me out in the smithy workshop which thankfully allowed Violet to take it easy now that she was looking after little Arthur. He was proving to be a handful indeed. Karl had become a good friend to me and Violet, and the girls had grown to love him as an uncle. He was also highly intelligent. With his aviation background he could visualise the benefits mobile radio communications would bring to aviation, especially in terms of safety, and he was extremely excited by it. I knew that of course, and he was right. His enthusiasm was infectious and his ability to take on information and new skills quickly was amazing. He wrote to his mother and father every week and I of course knew that he would have to go back to Germany at some point. We would all miss him terribly when that time came.

I walked up Ravens Lane whistling *It Must Be Love* by Madness and turned right into the top of George Street. All was quiet in the street and there didn't seem to be much going on at the workshop. I pushed open the smaller wooden door to the front of the workshop and stepped in. My eyes took a few seconds to adjust to the gloom inside, but I couldn't see or hear any activity, which was strange as I knew Karl was in this morning, I had left him working away at his bench earlier. I was just thinking that maybe he had gone out to the back to make his strange brew of Camp Coffee when I saw the body slumped against the far wall. With my stomach sinking and my heart racing I hurried over and managed to get down onto my one good knee beside Karl. I could see the huge blood stain all over the front of Karl's shirt, on his trousers and it was pooling on the floor between his legs. Judging by the large bubbles of blood slowly oozing out of the big hole in his chest I knew that this was a large calibre gunshot wound which had probably punched right through the lungs. I was no medical expert but I had seen enough at the front in Flanders to understand that in this day and age the wound was certainly fatal. Looking at it, it probably would have been back in 1984 too. I looked at his face. His skin was completely ashen in colour and his eyes were staring and lifeless.

'Karl, Karl, what happened? Who did this to you?'

Nothing.

'Karl, Karl, can you hear me?' I pleaded as I placed two of my fingers on the side of his neck. I had no idea what I was looking for but I had seen it done loads of times in the movies. I thought I heard something so I put my ear to his mouth. A faint whisper came from Karl's lips.

'George, Hauptmann Von Schultz, going to kill you. Going to your house.' I could barely hear it but I think I understood.

'A German, coming to kill me? Why Karl? Why?' I asked, looking into his eyes. There was no sign of life, just a tear running from his left eye down his cheek now. He had gone.

My first thought was the sinister soldier from 1984. Had he finally come back to get me? But why kill Karl? It didn't make any sense. My stomach was in knots and I thought I was going to throw up. How quickly your emotions can change I thought. I'd just gone from everything being all right in the world to everything being all wrong. I thought about Violet, the girls and little Arthur. They were at home; I had to get there quickly. I looked around for a weapon, anything that might do. There were many lethal tools in the smithy, but would they be of any use against a gun? I didn't think so. I picked up a large hammer anyway and hurried out of the workshop back into the bright summer light. I might be just a TV repair man and I might be lame, but I wasn't going to give up on my family and I now had Karl's death to avenge. Looking down and across the street all looked quiet at my house. I headed that way.

Reaching the front door, I could see that it was slightly ajar. That wasn't good. I pushed it open gently and listened carefully inside. Nothing, there was no sound at all coming from anywhere in the house. I stepped quietly into the hallway, making sure I kept my boots away from the hard linoleum and placed them only on the central carpet runner to deaden any sound. The parlour door on the left was open so I crept up and peered through the crack. There didn't appear to be anyone in the room but I couldn't be sure so I leaned very slowly into the room to get a better look. Nothing. Stepping back into the hallway I looked up the stairs, listening intently all the time, my heart racing. It was dark and very quiet. I reasoned that if I tried to walk up those creaky stairs I would be signalling my presence to anyone in the whole house, so I figured I would have to explore the ground floor living room and kitchen first. The living room door was shut, which was also very worrying. The living room door was never closed. I stood outside the door trying to control my breathing. My heart was hammering wildly in my chest and my nerves were screaming. There was nothing else for it, I had to go in there. I could hear the blood thumping in my ears as I put my cane down, leaning it against the wall, and put my right hand on the door knob, turning it slowly. The door creaked open a little. I peered through the small gap, but could see nothing, no movement and no sound. I pushed the door wide open then. I could see most of the room and it looked normal, nothing out of place. Feeling a little more confident now, I transferred the hammer into my sweating right hand and gripping it tightly I took one careful step into the room.

When it came, the explosion of pain in my left knee was indescribable. A big brown leather boot had stamped down hard on my left knee which sent a searing burning pain right up my left leg and instantly made me want to vomit. There was no way my lame right leg was going to hold me up so I went down hard onto my right side and rolled onto my back on the floor, pain screaming through my body. Looking up, I certainly didn't see what I was expecting. Instead of the sinister soldier I felt sure would be in my house, there was instead a tall British officer standing right behind the door. He had Violet in a headlock with his left arm and was holding a pistol to her head.

'Welcome George,' he smiled. 'Glad you could make it. Looks like someone tipped you off I was here?' he said, indicating the hammer which was now lying on the floor just to the left of my head. 'Was it Karl, is he still with us?' Von Schultz sneered.

His English was very good but I could still detect an accent, German I surmised. So Karl was right, it was a German who had killed him and was now inevitably going to do the same to me. But I still had no idea why.

'Who are you? What do you want? We've done nothing to you,' I pleaded.

'Yes I know,' retorted Von Schultz. 'But there are much bigger things happening here, things you wouldn't understand, and unfortunately you have to be eliminated. You've caused me more than a bit of trouble already George so I just want to get this finished now,' he said as he removed the muzzle of the revolver from Violet's head and aimed it down at me.

'I don't know who you are and what this is all about but please let my wife go. She has no part in any of this.'

I lay there with the gun pointed at me and I remember listening to the clock on the mantelpiece ticking loudly. Time seemed to have slowed right down, very probably ticking away the last moments of my life.

'Unfortunately she's got in the way though and she will cause a fuss once I've killed you, so it will be necessary to kill her also so I can get away cleanly,' he explained in a very cold and matter of fact way. His deep blue eyes showed no emotion whatsoever, there was no life in them, just coldness.

'As I said to poor Karl, it's not personal George, please do accept my apologies for this,' he said as he raised his right arm to point the muzzle of the revolver directly at my face. Time seemed to stand completely still for me now. Waiting. How could it all end like this? Just when I had started to really live life to the full. I finally had everything I had ever wanted, I had Violet and the girls to live for, to look after, and baby Arthur as well. It couldn't end like this, could it? What would happen when he pulled the trigger? Would I die in explosive agony here in the past or would I just suddenly find myself back in my flat in 1984. I knew then in that instant that I would rather die back here with Violet. I wouldn't live a life without her, I couldn't.

As all the questions ran through my head, Von Schultz put his thumb on the hammer and eased it back with a loud click. I could see his finger beginning to tighten around the trigger and my whole body tensed, waiting for the inevitable impact of the bullet. I didn't really mind dying, well of course I did, but I didn't seem to have very much choice in the matter anyway now, so there was no point getting stressed about it. What I was really upset about though was Violet. She was so loving, so sweet, she didn't deserve to die at the hands of this cold monster. I remembered being with her in the hospice in 1984, at the other end of her life. How could that be I wondered? If she was still alive in 1984 how could she die here with me in 1920? Well maybe she doesn't, maybe she somehow survives this? That thought made me feel a little better. Just then I was startled out of my slow motion reverie as Violet screamed and lunged violently at Von Schultz, pulling her head away from his arm and dragging her nails down his face whilst trying to grab the revolver with her other hand. The gun went off with a deafening explosion in the small room. Violet spun round in midair and then collapsed on the floor next to me, blood already pumping from her upper chest.

'Noooo!' I screamed as Violet's ashen face turned towards me and smiled.

'Sorry my love,' she whispered silently. 'I love you.'

'I love you too,' I whispered back, grabbing her hand and grasping it tight in mine. 'So much. Please don't leave me.'

'Stupid bitch!' screamed Von Schultz as he grabbed his face in pain. Blood was now flowing freely down his torn cheek. He kicked her hard in the ribs in temper. She didn't even notice. She was just lying there looking at me and I could see the last bubbles of air pumping from the large gaping hole in her chest and the life draining quickly out of her eyes. Her hand went limp in mine. I knew she had gone. Just like Karl.

'One bullet left now George and finally, this one's for you,' Von Schultz said as he raised his revolver again and aimed it down at me. At that moment I couldn't have cared less. I had lost my Violet.

Just then, I noticed a flash of black out of the corner of my eye. I couldn't comprehend what was happening, it seemed as if a giant black bat had suddenly appeared in the room and was now attacking Von Schultz. Von Schultz's right arm flew up into the air as the revolver went off, punching a large hole harmlessly through the ceiling. Howling loudly now, his head snapped violently back as the palm of a large white hand smashed upwards into his nose, spurting blood like a small fountain. That was followed by a knee which was slammed violently up into the German's soft groin. Von Schultz let out a load groan and as he doubled over the white hand connected again with his right temple while a second smashed into his throat. Von Schultz went down heavy with his head bouncing off the wall and again on the heavy wooden sideboard before he finally landed face down on the floor and laid still. It was all over in seconds. It was only then that I realised this wasn't in fact a large bat, or an apparition, my eyes began to focus and I could now see it was a very familiar, large and gangly dark cloaked figure. The sinister soldier from 1984.

'We have no time to lose,' he said as he knelt down next to Violet and put both of his hands over the large hole in her chest.

'What are you doing?' I asked, struggling now to sit up, but still gripping Violet's hand tightly.

'Please be quiet,' the strange cloaked man said softly, now with his eyes closed and obviously concentrating hard.

I had no idea what the hell was going on. How had he got in here and what did he think he was doing? And who was he?

I silently watched the pair of them for what seemed like ages. What else could I do? There was nothing I could do for my poor Violet and there was no phone for me to call for a doctor, who probably couldn't have done anything for her anyway. It was out of my hands now and it did look like whatever the sinister soldier was doing, he was obviously trying to help her. I just sat there holding her limp hand while the cloaked man clasped his hands on the wound and continued to concentrate hard, his face creased in tension.

I had my eyes closed tightly now, trying to stop the stinging tears rolling down my cheeks. I couldn't lose her now, not when I had got everything I ever wanted. I loved her and the children so much. I was sinking into despair.

Just then Violet's hand suddenly grasped mine. Did I dream it? No, she gripped it tightly again. I opened my watery eyes and stared down at her. Her deep green eyes were looking at me and they were smiling. She mouthed 'I love you.' I did the same back, tears now streaming down my face.

The cloaked man finally opened his eyes and released his hands from Violet's chest.

'She's going to be OK George,' he said simply. He then moved away from Violet and grabbed something from under his cloak. He turned to Von Schultz who was still laying there unmoving, blood running from his nose and a nasty gash in his forehead. His breathing was ragged and laboured. Probably something to do with the deep crimson bruise which was now appearing on his throat I thought, with not a small amount of pleasure. The cloaked man grabbed both Von Schultz's hands and roughly pulled them behind his back. Within seconds he had bound both hands with a plastic cable tie. He then did the same with his ankles.

'There, that should hold him. Plastic ties, not quite 1920s eh George? Hopefully no one will notice?'

'Who are you?' I asked.

'All in good time George. Let's get things tidied up here and then we can talk. Violet is going to be fine.'

He laid his hand on her tummy. 'Your baby son is fine too,' he said with a big smile that creased his whole face. 'All Violet needs is rest, we need to get her to bed.'

'Baby? What baby?' I stammered, looking down at Violet, the big hole in her chest now miraculously gone, just leaving her blood stained torn dress as evidence of the trauma.

'Oh, sorry George, didn't you know? Damn. I shouldn't have mentioned it,' said the cloaked man. 'Where are the other children?' he asked.

That was the first time I had thought of them since the fight with Von Schultz had started. 'Oh my God, I don't know. I guess they must be with their Nan, Violet's mother. I hope so.'

'OK, good,' said the cloaked man as he stood up. Just then Violet whispered something.

'Sorry love, I didn't hear you,' I said, putting my ear close to her lips.

'George, the children are with Sarah, they will be fine. How are you?' she asked, gripping my hand tightly again.

'I'm fine my love, let's just get you to bed and looked after,' I said softly, smiling at her.

The cloaked man reached down and grabbed my hand to help me up. It was a bit of a struggle. I hadn't realised just how much pain I still had in my good leg, the one Von Schultz had stamped on. I eventually made it up on two feet, with the cloaked man's help, and he passed me my walking stick.

'Thank you sir, whoever you are. You saved Violet and me too. I don't know how or why, but at the moment I don't really care, we're alive,' I said.

'Don't worry about that,' said the cloaked man. 'For now we just need to get Violet into bed and rested. I have fixed her body but she has lost a fair bit of blood. I'm not able to replace that, her body is going to have to do that by itself now. We need to get her mother back here and she can look after her and she will need a lot of tender loving care for a few days.'

With that, the cloaked man bent down and scooped Violet up in his arms as if she weighed no more than a baby. He then carried her to the door and up the stairs.

'Which is your bedroom?' shouted the cloaked figure down the stairs.

'Along the landing, right at the front,' I shouted back.

I was leaning against the hallway wall when he came back down. He put his big hand on my shoulder and looked down into my eyes.

'George, the worst is over. We can breathe again now for a while. We need to get Mr Evil in there out of your house and I feel certain that the authorities will want to have a serious little chat with him. I don't fancy his chances much, so I don't think you'll have to worry about him again. I expect he'll be facing the firing squad soon enough. I'll get things all sorted with the authorities, don't worry on that score. George, can you go and get the doctor to check over Violet and the baby. Oh, on second thoughts perhaps don't mention the baby to Violet or the doctor, maybe she doesn't know yet. Oh, wait perhaps we should first get Karl into bed, he needs lots of rest too?'

I stared at the cloaked man in shock. I had forgotten about poor Karl.

'But he died, he died in front of me, I saw him.'

'Yes George, but I did manage to get there in time, just. That's why I was slightly late in getting here. I hadn't expected to have to cut it so fine, I'm sorry about that, but I had to stop and save Karl first. You see, I can fix these things but I have to do it very quickly. If someone has passed over for too long I can't get them back.'

I just stood there gaping at the cloaked man, uncomprehendingly.

'Now George, don't try to work it all out, let's just do it. I'll take Von Schultz over and dump him in the workshop for now, and I'll bring Karl back and put him to bed. You go and get the doctor and get your mother-in-law and make sure the children are okay. I'll leave you to try and make up a suitable story for all of them. I suggest you tell them Violet and Karl have both come down with the flu or something like that. After the pandemic of last year that will be serious enough for the doctor to want to come straight over. We'll have to ask Karl and Violet not to discuss what happened with anyone just yet. I'll then get down to the post office and get a message to my contacts in the security forces and get Von Schultz dealt with. After that, you and I can sit down with a nice cuppa. We have a lot to discuss.'

With that he went back into the living room to collect the still unconscious German. He picked him up and threw the body over his shoulder as easily as he had picked Violet up. I was amazed at his apparent strength, it was inhuman. Just who or what was he? I guessed I was about to find out soon enough. At least I hoped so, I had had enough of all this, I needed some answers. With that thought I hurried out behind him, closing the door behind me.

Violet and Karl were finally settled and comfortable in bed and Violet's mum was fussing over the pair of them. In fact, if I was honest I was beginning to think Sarah had a bit of a soft spot for Karl. I'd definitely have to keep an eye on that one; I don't think he'd know what had hit him if Sarah decided she was going to have her wicked way with him. Karl was a bright guy but he was clueless as far as women were concerned. The girls and little Arthur were now over at my Mum and Dad's having tea. They loved it over there as my parents doted on them.

I had just made a pot of tea and had taken it into the front parlour where the cloaked man and I were making ourselves comfortable. He had been over at the workshop dealing with the military police and had just returned. He didn't say much about it but it was clear that the authorities wanted Von Schultz very much and were extremely grateful that we had captured him. I hoped the cloaked man hadn't forgotten to take off the cable ties before he handed Von Schultz over.

The cloaked man sat in the big leather armchair next to the fireplace and I sat on the sofa with my leg up.

'Well you have me at a disadvantage,' I said. 'You know my name, you know my family, you know a great deal about me and you seem to know what's going on. I don't even know your name.'

'Yes that's true and I do have to apologise for that, but I will try to make amends and explain as much as I can,' said the cloaked man.

'Thank you,' I said, taking a large gulp of tea and thinking I might need something a little stronger before this conversation was finished.

'Firstly, let's get the introductions out of the way. You would not be able to pronounce my name as it is in my own tongue, so we can forget that. I have been known by many names throughout the years, but mostly I have been known as Machidiel by your people. That's still a bit of a mouthful so you can call me Mac.'

'Mac? That's it? It's not too exotic for a time travelling god like you is it?' I laughed.

'Yes, that's it, Mac. Nice and simple isn't it?' he grinned.

'Yes I guess so,' I agreed. 'Go on then Mac, spill the beans.'

'Well, it's all a bit complicated, I'm not sure where to start without you getting even more confused.'

'Why don't you start with the old lady Violet in 1984? Why were you there and why did you follow me to my flat and then somehow spirit me back to 1918?' I suggested.

'Yes OK. But that's not a good place to start George. It's all very much bigger than that.' It was obvious that Mac was struggling to explain this in any way that was going to be easy for me to understand. 'Look, let me try and simplify this. George Putnam was born in 1894. He met Violet, fell in love and married her on Christmas day 1912. He went off to war in August 1915. He was supposed to get a knee wound but still survive the war and come home to Violet, but he didn't you see. He died out there in no-man's-land and he shouldn't have. That wasn't supposed to happen and that's where it all started to go wrong.'

'What do you mean, that wasn't supposed to happen? How do you know it wasn't supposed to happen to him?' I asked.

'Mmm, let me come back to that one later. If you can, just accept for now that we know that's how it was supposed to happen.' Mac leaned forward in his chair and took a piece of shortbread and dipped it in his tea. 'You see, when events don't go how they are supposed to, when things are changed, however small those things might seem at the time, there can be massive consequences later on. George was supposed to survive the war in France but something was changed and he didn't, and that had dire consequences. Those consequences ultimately impacted on hundreds of thousands of people and even whole nations. They were the consequences that I was sent here to fix, to put back to how they were supposed to be.'

'So are you talking about the theory of changing small things in the past which have a massive effect in the future? I've read many novels that use that theme, but it's not true is it? It can't happen?'

'Yes George, it can happen, and unfortunately it does happen far too often. That's why I'm here, to put those events right when they go wrong.'

'But I'm confused, who are you? The time police or something?'

Mac laughed. 'Yes, something like that George, that's quite a good description.'

'OK, Mac, let's assume for now I accept that, what does all this have to do with me? Why did you bring me back here from 1984? Was it just to stand in for George?

'But that's just it George, and I know you are going to struggle to get your head around this, but you didn't come back to replace George Puttnam, you are George Puttnam.'

'But that's impossible,' I laughed. 'How can I be George Puttnam? As you said, he was born in 1894. I was born in 1960.'

'Yes George, you were born in 1894, you died in 1918 when you shouldn't have, and then you were reborn again in 1960.'

'But that's absurd. Are you saying that everyone who dies gets reborn again? Like reincarnation or something?' I asked.

'Yes, in a way. It's a bit more complicated than that but in essence that's it yes. That's how life works George. All life, across the universe, in fact across all universes. It always has. Of course your scientists haven't worked all this out yet George, but they are getting close. One or two of your older, eastern civilisations have unwittingly stumbled across some of the universal truths of life and have known about these for thousands of years, but your western civilisations have largely dismissed those beliefs. You see, there are in essence only about fifty life sources which are the source of all life across all universes. Those life forces have been there since the beginning of time, and from before any universe was even formed. In fact, as dictated by the laws of quantum physics, without these life forces the universes couldn't even have come into existence in the first place. Each of these separate life forces reproduce themselves again and again and are born and reborn as humans, animals, insects and all of the numerous other life forms we have across all universes. This is why all life forms everywhere are interconnected through these fifty basic life sources, which in fact form the very fabric of the universe. So you see the whole universe is connected. Your eastern traditions got that bit right. In your scientific terms you could look at the life source as a sort of transmitter and our brains are just receivers and amplifiers for the consciousness that is intrinsic to the fabric of space-time. You can look at your own consciousness as a form of unique bar-code George. Everything that lives has its own bar-code but is linked to the central life source. Your bar-code cannot be destroyed George, when you die the energy of your consciousness just gets recycled back into a different body at some point. Your life was extinguished in George Puttnam in 1918 and your consciousness was then reborn again in the newborn baby George Gade in 1960. But that one was never really meant to be, it was tampered with, so we were able to reverse it.'

I looked at Mac as he took a fourth piece of shortbread biscuit from the plate and dunked it into the remains of his tea. He noticed me looking at him.

'Sorry, I have sweet tooth,' he apologised. Then he continued.

'Anyway, the problem we had was to find out exactly where and when your reborn life force would pop up as we are never sure about that. We had a good lead though; Violet. Due to the quantum laws of entanglement, individual life forces, or bar-codes if you like, tend to become entwined with each other and are reborn again and again in an entwined state. That causes individual lives down through the centuries to become inextricably linked with each other. We knew therefore that your life force would be linked to Violet's life force and would inevitably pop up again somewhere around her. All we had to do was watch and wait for it to happen, and be there when it did. The real problem we had was that we could only reverse the change that had occurred whilst Violet was still alive and then we could go back and change things. If Violet had died before we found you and her life force had moved on and been reborn somewhere else in another time, or another universe, then things would become irrevocable and the change in time would have become permanent. We watched Violet her whole life and we were becoming somewhat concerned when she contracted cancer and was obviously approaching the end and we still hadn't spotted you, until that day in the hospice of course.'

'And on that point, why were you dressed in a soldier's uniform?' I asked.

'Ah.' Mac smiled. 'That's an easy one to explain. It was simply because I had just been back to the Somme in 1918 when George Puttnam died to look for more clues, to see if we had missed anything. We were getting a bit desperate you see.'

'And why was I reborn over forty years later? Why the long wait? Why not straightaway?'

'Well.' Mac paused, obviously trying to think of words to use that I would understand. 'Time is all relative. You are talking of forty years in earth related time, that's how you see it based here on this planet, but in reality each moment in time is always here, there is no concept of past and future, in a universal sense there was no gap of forty years, it was simply just another point in time and space.'

I think that explanation confused me even more and I was definitely struggling to grasp all of this. 'OK,' I said, now leaning forward on the sofa. 'Assuming all that is true, what is so important about me? And why did things change? Or perhaps more importantly, who changed them?

Mac leaned back in his chair. He took a pipe out of his pocket and a small penknife out of the other and began to scrape the pipe bowl.

'Do you mind if I smoke?'

'No not at all, I'll get you an ashtray. Do you fancy a proper drink?' I asked as I stood up and leaned heavily on my stick.

'Mmm that would be nice, what have you got?'

'I have a nice whisky I save for special occasions. I think this might be one of them.'

'That would be grand.' Mac smiled.

I went over to the mahogany cabinet and opened the ornately carved door. I pulled out a new centenary bottle of Johnnie Walker Gold Label whisky and two cut crystal glasses and placed them on the top of the cabinet where I poured two healthy shots out. I grabbed a King George V victory ashtray from the top of the sideboard and placed it down on the arm of Mac's chair along with his whisky.

'Thank you George, most kind. Cheers,' Mac said, raising his glass to me.

'Cheers Mac, and thank you again from the bottom of my heart for saving Violet and Karl. How did you do that by the way? Don't worry, just tell me, you can't shock me anymore, just tell me if you're actually a god or something?'

'A god? No hardly.' Mac giggled. 'But I'm not human if that's what you are asking. I come from an ancient civilisation which is not even of this particular universe, but that is a whole other story George. In my world we have learned to manipulate energy using our thought processes alone. If you have read your Einstein you will know that energy is matter at the molecular level so we can manipulate just about anything. My people became extremely good at manipulating bio matter and healing tissue and bone damage when required. We can fix many illnesses and sometimes even bring bodies back to life, as long as they are only very recently passed over, before the life force has actually left. After fifteen or twenty minutes or so it's usually too late and the bar-code has gone. After that there's nothing I can do. That was why I had to fix Karl before I came to you. I took a chance there and it was touch and go for a while.'

'So what you're saying is you can heal just by putting your hands on someone and using your mental powers to repair all the damage back to how it was before the damage occurred?'

'Yes that's about it,' smiled Mac.

'So have you had to do this before?' I asked.

'Yes many times, throughout the various universes and here on earth too. Many times in your history I have been here and fixed events, and people, like I did Violet and Karl. Mostly I am able to keep it all very quiet but occasionally there are witnesses and these have led to stories being told and even legends created. I was always amused when people referred to me as a god or an angel and even one or twice as a wizard. I suppose to their primitive viewpoint I was something otherworldly of course, it was perhaps the only way they could understand it. I believe I even deserved a number of mentions in your great book the Bible.' Mac grinned.

I just looked at Mac, stunned. My whole view of the world and the universe was unravelling before me.

'So back to my question, what is so important about me, why did things change and who changed them?' I asked.

Mac struck a match and started to light his pipe, drawing in the aromatic smoke through his mouth and out through his nostrils. I hadn't actually smoked a cigarette since the day I arrived home. Violet didn't frown upon it but she didn't smoke herself. Even though smoking was actually encouraged as a healthy pastime in this era, I knew the realities of passive smoking so I had no intention of smoking in front of the children, so I had just given up. Mind you, watching Mac with his pipe I was tempted to light up again. I took another swig of whisky instead.

'You don't know it yet but you are extremely important George. In fact, world changing important. Your death had as much impact on this planet as say the untimely death of John Fitzgerald Kennedy.'

'You have got to be joking?' I said, astounded. 'I'm just a TV repair man.'

'No, believe me it's true,' said Mac, puffing on his cigar and carefully blowing perfect rings of smoke upwards towards the ceiling.

'Your unplanned death brought about some significant changes to this world which would have become permanent, if we hadn't found you in time and reversed it.'

'I don't believe you. You're going to have to explain that one,' I said, taking another large swig of my whisky, letting the soft, smooth liquor slide down my throat and feeling the warmth spread into my chest.

'George, even if I knew, I wouldn't tell you everything that's going to happen to you in your life, for your own sake. Well not in any great detail anyway. Believe me, it's better not to know, it would send you mad. It's much better to let your life unfold, just like everyone else. And I'm talking about this life, the one here and now with Violet, I'm not talking about the life you had in 1984, that was a mistake, it just wasn't meant to happen and anyway, it no longer exists, it never happened. However, you have been to the future and we can't change that, it's not like the men in black where we can simply erase your memory or anything like that. So you know more than any other man alive at this moment in time George. You will always be different and you will have to learn to live with that, well at least up until 1984 anyway, if you live that long.' Mac smiled.

'I know you will cope OK, you are very resourceful George. I will however tell you enough so that you can understand how important you are and why we had to reverse things. It will also be necessary so that you can watch out for yourself in the future. The danger hasn't passed fully yet.'

I gave Mac a worried look.

'George, in a nutshell, in this life you go on to work with Marconi and others to further develop the science of radio. Your friendship with Karl is also extremely important. As you are aware, Karl is very well educated in the theories of flight and has become quite fascinated, sorry no, quite obsessive, with the burgeoning new aviation industry. With your knowledge of radio and his knowledge of aviation, you and he successfully develop the first land to air and air to land radio communications. You also both go on to develop a method for successfully jamming radio signals over a wide area. It is this particular development that turns the tide of the Battle of Britain in the coming Second World War in Great Britain's favour. The Germans used radio waves to direct their bombers onto their targets in 1940. This process was really quite accurate and without your jamming of the signals the Germans would have been able to more precisely bomb the RAF targets, which would have put the whole RAF out of the war during August 1940 and allow the planned German land operation Sea-Lion to take place in September.'

I was almost speechless. I couldn't believe what Mac was telling me. My work was going to help Britain win the Second World War? I just couldn't see how that was at all possible.

'Mac, I just don't see that. That's not what happened was it?'

'George, that's just the point. That is what was supposed to have happened, in the normal time line, and will happen now that you are back here alive and well. Obviously during your twenty four years or so after you were reborn in 1960 the change had already taken place, so that was not the history you knew was it?'

'No Mac it wasn't,' I agreed. 'Germany won the war, not Britain and France.'

'And what did that mean for you living in England George?'

'Well, it wasn't too bad. We were of course governed from Berlin, as was the rest of Europe, the Middle East, Africa and parts of Asia. As long as we adhered to the rules things were safe enough though. Of course, if you spoke out against the regime or if you were an undesirable, things could get difficult.'

'In what way George?'

'Well, we all knew that people went missing if they spoke out and were most often never seen again. I learned in my history lessons that all of the Jews, Poles, Russians and Gypsies were removed early on so I never saw any of them. Black people were only allowed to do manual labour, even though I knew many of them and they were far more capable than that. I always disliked that rule. Britain is a big industrialised manufacturing nation in 1984. We supplied the Reich with our technologies, and we manufactured thousands of trucks and military vehicles for them, and of course food from agriculture, and oil and gas from the North Sea, so there were loads of opportunities, but not really for black people. There was a law preventing them from having an education.'

'Let me ask you something George. What happened to any handicapped children in your 1984?'

'Handicapped children? That's a strange question. Well there weren't any that I knew of, they were disposed of at birth of course.'

'Of course? Didn't you think that was an unpleasant way to deal with a human life George?'

'I don't know Mac, I've not thought much about it before.' And I really hadn't to be truthful. But now that I had started to discuss it with Mac I felt very uncomfortable about it all. I had a difficult childhood growing up in a children's care home so I could fully appreciate what being the underdog and being persecuted felt like. Mac was right; there were a lot of unpleasant things about the society I had grown up in during the 1970s and 80s. The society here in 1920, despite the war and the high levels of poverty, seemed much more open and less oppressive somehow. If I could change that future I had, I would sure like to try I thought.

'But thinking about it Mac, I agree with a lot of what you have said, and the future you have suggested is the correct one sounds infinitely better than the one I knew. But tell me, if it all goes back to how it should have been, will all the people I knew cease to exist or anything like that?'

Mac laughed. 'No, the life forms will still all be there in one form or another but it is true that their actual lives will almost certainly be different. What you need to think about George is that this is the way history should have been, not the one that you remember, that was false.'

'Yes Mac, I understand. But tell me, who tried to change it? Who wanted me dead in 1918 and why?'

'Mmmm that's another complicated one George, but I'll try and fill you in as best as I can. It was a very long time ago when one of my kind went bad. He was often known by your people as Azael, which is as good a name as any. He turned away from the work we were doing to keep all of the time streams on track and started to change things to suit himself. It wasn't for any type of personal gain or anything like that. You see, we have everything that we could ever want and money and possessions have no value for us. But when you have lived as long as we do and have seen as much as we have, boredom and repetition is our main enemy. He has become somewhat deranged and he plays around with time for fun, for his own personal pleasures. He has been focused on the earth for some time now and for some reason he seems to obtain some sort of perverse satisfaction in playing around with your people more than any other. He began by making some big changes, but we were able to detect those very easily when we discovered what he was up to, and we managed to put things right again fairly quickly. But he got wise to the fact that we were now monitoring things much more closely so he started to make more subtle changes which were very much harder to detect, but which still had a large impact further down that particular time line. It has become a game with him you see, a game of cat and mouse with us.'

'That's a particularly nasty game Mac, one that destroys people's lives?'

'Yes, he is pure evil George. He has no feelings for any other living being, to him you are all just insects in a jar to be tormented and played with for his own amusement.'

'Nice.'

'So, as I said, he likes to make subtle changes to catch us out, and one such subtle change he made involved you George. In the correct time line it seems that you met Karl in no-man's-land that day you were shot in the knee, and he assisted you back to your own lines. He was taken prisoner and you were sent back home. You met up again when Karl came to see you in your home town in 1919 and the rest, as they say, is history. Azael knew this so he enlisted the help of that nasty piece of work, Von Schultz, to make sure you and Karl were both killed in no-man's-land. He reasoned that with all those millions of other deaths taking place we wouldn't notice a couple more. Which we didn't immediately and we very nearly missed it. From what we can make out, it seems that Von Schultz was unable to find you that day, but he had already made sure he had Karl very much where he wanted him, in his own platoon, under his control. He was under strict instructions from Azael to kill at least one of you to stop you both meeting up and inventing the radio jamming device which prevented the Nazis from winning the Second World War. When he couldn't find you, he decided to just kill Karl. When he shot Karl he didn't realise that it was only a glancing blow to the side of his head, it knocked him unconscious but didn't kill him. As luck would have it though, or bad luck in your case, because of quantum entanglement he fell into the shell hole that you were already laying in. You were always destined to meet in that particular shell hole, one way or the other, if only Von Schultz had known that. Unfortunately, instead of saving you, as this time he was unconscious, Karl fell in on top of you and pushed your head under the water, where in your weakened state you drowned.

So although Von Schultz messed up killing Karl, he inadvertently managed to kill you. Azael wouldn't have known that, but he did know that his desired changes had come about so he was happy, well of course until now that is.'

'What will he do now that you have returned things to how they should be Mac?'

'I don't think we can really say George. It may be that now he knows that we know about this little scheme he will also know that we will continue to monitor the situation closely. He may therefore give up on it and go and play somewhere else. Alternatively, he might also take it as a challenge and try again. He seems to have a fixation lately in altering things to ensure Hitler and his Nazis win the Second World War, so I'm sure he will inevitably be up to something. That's our little problem though. We will be monitoring the time lines carefully around this period for some time to come I think.'

I sat back in my chair and watched Mac drain his last drop of whisky.

'Fancy another?' I asked.

'Yes, why not, one for the road then?' He smiled.

'For an angel you're not too angelic are you?' I quipped.

Mac laughed heartily as he let out some more smoke and formed a few more rings. 'No I guess I'm not.'

'So what about Violet, me and the children? Are we safe?' I asked.

Mac contemplated this for a while. 'Yes, reasonably so. As I said, we shall be monitoring events quite closely so I don't think you have too much to worry about, but you should just remain on your guard, at least until the events of the 1939 to 1945 war have played out.'

'OK, and one last thing,' I said.

'Yes, what's that?' asked Mac.

'I don't have to go back now to 1984 or anywhere else? This life with Violet is my life, forever?'

'Yes George, it is, forever. It is your life.' Mac smiled.

I walked quietly up the stairs and stepped into the darkened front bedroom. I could hear Violet's steady breathing in the half-light so I went and stood over by the bed, just to be near her. I don't know quite how long I stood there like that. I was just so happy, this was the life I had always wanted, I had always dreamed about. I loved Violet so much. I tried not to think too much about what the future might hold for us, the girls, little Arthur and our yet to be born little boy, I just wanted to enjoy the here and now. Satisfied that Violet was sleeping soundly I turned to walk away.

'I love you George.'

I turned back and sat on the bed next to her. Her hand found mine and squeezed it, sending a flutter throughout my whole body.

'I love you too Violet. I always will.'

'Are we safe now George?'

'Yes Violet, we are safe now,' I promised, and smiled.

Chapter Fifteen

Epilogue – December 1945

Well, old Mac the not so angelic angel was right of course. Karl and I did eventually get to go into business with Marconi, developing ever better and better radio sets. Even though I say it myself, we were very good at what we did, which was perhaps unsurprising given my futuristic knowledge. I'm almost ashamed to admit that we also made ourselves quite rich in the process. I was in at the start of broadcasting with Marconi and the BBC as I had planned, and those were exciting times indeed. The Second World War has come and gone and as a direct result of my and Karl's efforts we managed to stop the Luftwaffe from decimating the RAF in 1940. I served as a Captain in the army, attached directly to the war office and spent many an exciting time in the cabinet war rooms under Whitehall in London. I managed to celebrate V.E. day with Violet in Piccadilly Circus, and, I am pleased to say, I was dressed in uniform again. I can't recall how many girls I kissed that day, but of course I ended up in Violet's arms. Never one to learn from my mistakes, I ate too much cake again and Violet had to put me to bed.

As Karl had predicted, Great Britain and her allies have indeed won the war. From here on in, I have no certain idea as to what the future holds as it may have changed significantly now from any history I ever learned back in my 1970s and 80s. That's a good thing as far as I'm concerned.

Violet and I have two beautiful daughters and two doting sons who, to our great relief, all managed to get through the war unscathed. Albert and young Mac both fought in Europe with distinction. Daisy and Albert now work with me in our hi-tech business developing the new transistor radio and the latest television sets. I have already designed and produced a far too futuristic colour TV set with a remote control. I don't think the world is quite ready for it just yet, but I feel sure we will launch it when the time is right, and obviously just before anyone else invents it. I've also got some thoughts about assisting NASA with communications on a little project to the moon they might have in the 1960s, but that's quite a few years ahead yet. I must remember to buy those shares in McDonald's too.

Evelyn and young Mac are both rising stars in the BBC and are doing extremely well. As a married female Evelyn is finding it difficult on occasions; it's hardly Nazi Germany but there are still far too many prejudices for my liking. I step in when I can but Evelyn always scolds me for it. She is certainly her own woman.

Karl managed to get the rest of his family out of Germany in the 1930s before the Nazis took a firm hold and they've all settled here in England now, and are very happy. Karl and I are still partners in the business although he tends to run our aviation research division side of things. His work with the MOD takes up most of his time of late. He did finally manage to escape the clutches of Sarah and find time to settle down with a lovely English wife, Rosalyn, just before the war and they now have two beautiful girls. It has to be said that without our work with the MOD I think Karl and some of his family might have found themselves locked up in internment camps here in Britain during the war. However, he was far too valuable to the allied war effort for that, so strings were pulled everywhere to ensure they were kept out.

Violet and I are still madly in love. I believe we always will be. We have our first wonderful granddaughter now and life just continues to get better and better. My thoughts do wander sometimes to the events of 1984, my 1984, and back to those eventful days at the end of the First World War. I haven't seen Mac, my angel of time since that day in our front parlour, but I have always suspected that he was around somewhere, keeping an eye on things. I am hoping that with the successful outcome to the war this time, I can breathe a little easier now.

So, all's well that end's well as they say.

Oh and I nearly forgot to mention, Mr Churchill has nominated me for a knighthood. Not bad for a TV repair man eh?

A thank you from the Author

Time is the most valuable commodity we humans possess. None of us know how long we have left, it may be years or it may be months, but whatever it is there is one thing that we can all be certain of, we never have enough time. That is why I want to personally thank you from the bottom of my heart for the amount of your highly valued time you have already invested in reading this book. Thank you. Now, in common with all new independent authors, my stories will either live or die depending on the amount of feedback they receive. It is a fact in this on-line digital age we now live in, that without feedback many products simply won't be purchased and books won't be bought without adequate on-line feedback. So, before you go, can I ask you please to invest just a little bit more of your time and write a short review for this book on Amazon? Just a few sentences is all that is required and your comments will add to the story. Please, this really matters. Feedback means everything to me as an author and I do indeed read every review.

If you wish you can also drop me a line info@michael-stewart.net and I will be happy to respond or you can visit my website at www.michael-stewart.net

Thank you most sincerely and I hope to see you soon in another story.

Michael Stewart

Lightning Source UK Ltd.
Milton Keynes UK
UKOW05f1930170317
296937UK00004B/235/P